NAPACHEE

24964

NAPACHEE

A NOVEL BY

ROBERT FEAGAN

An imprint of
Beach Holme Publishing
Vancouver, B.C.

This book is published by Beach Holme Publishing, #226—2040
West 12th Ave., Vancouver, BC, V6J 2G2. This is a Sandcastle
Book. Teacher's guide available from Beach Holme Publishing,
call toll-free 1-888-551-6655.

We acknowledge the financial support
of the Canada Council for the Arts,
the Government of Canada through
the Book Publishing Industry
Development Program (BPIDP) and
the assistance of the Province of
British Columbia through the British
Columbia Arts Council for our
publishing activities and program.

THE CANADA COUNCIL | LE CONSEIL DES ARTS
FOR THE ARTS | DU CANADA
SINCE 1957 | DEPUIS 1957

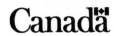

Canadä

Editor: Joy Gugeler
Cover Illustration: Julia Bell
Production and Cover Design: Teresa Bubela
Text Design: Jen Hamilton

Canadian Cataloguing in Publication Data

Feagan, Robert, 1959-
  Napachee

  "A Sandcastle Book."
  ISBN 0-88878-403-I

  1. Inuit--Juvenile fiction. I. Title.
PS8561.E18N36 1999   jC813'.54   C99-910880-8
PZ7.F2935Na 1999

To my grandfather, Chester Feagan,
and to my parents Hugh and Marj
who nourished my vivid imagination.

ONE

The young polar bear lifted its head and sniffed the breeze as it swept across the barren expanse of the arctic tundra. It was an incredible July morning; the eternal darkness of a long northern winter had faded into a brilliant northern "spring". The cub stood on its hind legs struggling to identify the strange scent that floated on the wind. It carried fear and adventure and the discovery of things unseen. Returning to all fours, the cub timidly set forward.

Suddenly, a low reproachful growl startled the cub so that it turned to acknowledge its mother approaching and scampered to her side. She continued to scold it for wandering too far from sight, nuzzling it with her nose and flipping it over onto its back. Her mouth opened, large and tongue-filled, and she licked the cub's small, angular face. With one more nudge she pushed it back onto its feet and toward the water.

The cub's mother slowly but gracefully followed behind her young one, stopping only to take a deep breath of the breeze. She knew the smell of man and the danger that could travel with it. She would not feel secure until that scent was far, far away.

❄

Napachee held his breath. He closed his left eye, looked along the sight and pulled the trigger. The rifle shot rang in his ears as he realized he had, in fact, closed *both* eyes. He heard his father's soft laughter and knew his shot had not been a good one. Chuckling, his father pointed at the target they had set up on the snow some yards away. Napachee looked at it closely only to find that there was no mark on it at all! He had missed it completely!

"You must be patient," Enuk said. "You are too anxious to shoot and do not think. Keep both of your hands steady and squeeze the trigger slowly. We have been hunting these lands for many years and it is our *patience* that has helped us survive. You will learn this patience as I did, and your grandfather before me."

Enuk looked at his son. Napachee had handsome traditional Inuit features: his straight black hair and wide cheekbones framed dark, wide-set almond eyes and a broad, but finely chiseled, nose. He had a strong stocky build, with broad shoulders and muscular arms and legs. His dark skin was tanned from the spring sun reflecting off of the arctic snow. Enuk looked like an older version of his son, though he had shorter hair and a set, determined mouth.

Napachee and his father had been out on the land for almost a week, hunting and camping as they went. Caribou were nearby, and they had been following them patiently. High in the treeless tundra, the wind seemed never-ending as it blew across the open expanse, but it packed the snow into a hard covering that supported a fully-loaded snowmobile and sled.

In the dead of winter the sun disappeared and the land was enveloped in twenty-four hours of darkness, but it was now July and the first signs of the arctic spring had begun to show themselves. It was only -10 today, and the sun was shining brightly off the snowy crystals beneath Napachee's feet. Both father and son wore caribou parkas, mittens and pants, warm woolly socks and fur boots called *kamiks*, each item made by Napachee's mother. Normally, he felt happy to be out with his father, but he had other things on his mind.

"What if I can *never* learn to be patient?" Napachee asked. "What if I can *never* become the great hunter you think I will be?"

"You will learn," Enuk said softly, smiling. "You will learn and you will feel the same pride all your ancestors felt before you."

"What if I do not wish to learn?" Napachee blurted. "What if I do not wish to be a hunter?"

"What is it? Why do you speak this way?" Enuk said, a worried expression on his face.

Napachee was almost fourteen. He had known for some time that he was not interested in the land and the hunt. When he was younger he had loved going out with his father. Despite what he had just said he knew he was already a very good hunter, but now at night, when he lay awake in bed, he dreamed of greater things; things that were only found in large cities. He had seen these cities on TV and read about them in school. He was fascinated by what he might find there and eager for adventure.

"I do not have the love of the land that you have," Napachee said quietly. "I have outgrown the North, and I have outgrown the hunt. I want to see a city, to live there, to experience something different."

Enuk scowled at his son. He had sensed recently that Napachee was growing distant. From a young age his son had reminded Enuk of his own father. The boy had always been at home on the land and possessed a gift for tracking animals where others could not. To Enuk's dismay this had changed in the last year.

"You will be a hunter!" Enuk replied firmly. "We have always been hunters and we always will be hunters! Do not argue with me."

"But Father, I cannot...."

"That is enough!" Enuk scolded firmly. "I do not want to hear any more of this nonsense. Help me load the sled and we will go home."

They loaded the equipment from the igloo they had built for shelter onto the low flat sled, a *komatik* in silence. As his father hitched the dogs, Napachee fastened their belongings to it in preparation to leave. The dogs tugged excitedly against the fan hitch at the front of the sled and spread out across the hard packed snow in anticipation of the journey. With a soft click of Enuk's tongue, the dogs lunged ahead while both father and son jogged along side. The *komatik* sped up and Napachee slid on behind his father.

Napachee fought back tears on the bumpy ride home. His father was blind! The world had changed and his father still wanted to live in the past. Everything his father did frustrated Napachee. He tried to understand his father, but it the harder he tried the harder it became. They seemed to live in two different worlds. Forty years ago, his father had been born on the land near Cambridge Bay on Victoria Island. He was Inuit and spoke Inuktitut. Cambridge Bay was a small community of only a thousand people, and although it had seemed small, it had been home to Napachee until two years ago.

When Napachee had turned twelve, his father had decided to move west to Sachs Harbour, on Banks Island where people were less influenced by the ways of the South. Sachs Harbour was even smaller than Cambridge Bay! People who lived here were Inuvialuit and spoke a different dialect called Inuvialuktun.

Napachee could speak Inuktitut fluently and the Inuvialuktun dialect was very similar so he could understand and speak it well enough to communicate. But all of his new friends, even if they could speak their own Inuvialuktun dialect, spoke English at school and at the game hall.

Napachee's father spoke to him in Inuktitut and expected Napachee to answer him in the same fashion.

Enuk's distant relatives had been a mix of Inuvialuit and Inuit and he had hoped the move to Sachs Harbour would bring his family closer to the culture shared by both regions.

And if language wasn't enough to set him apart, there were also his father's old-fashioned ways. Most people used canvas tents when they went hunting, wore parkas bought at the local Co-op store and used snowmobiles to speed across the ice. Napachee's father insisted on chopping snow blocks to build igloos while they were out on the land, wore caribou clothing fashioned by Napachee's mother and used dog sleds to go hunting.

As they made the bumpy journey home, Napachee gazed out across the sea ice. His face was hot from the sun and snow, and sleep began to drift over him. A comfortable darkness wrapped around his thoughts, and enveloped him in a dream world. Napachee felt himself drifting toward a faint light in the distance. In the dream the brightness grew stronger and became the beckoning lights of a city far off on the horizon.

❄

As the days passed, the sun lifted itself higher above the horizon in one continuous sunset: orange, pink and blue. The polar bear cub could see *Okpik*, the snowy owl soaring high above in search of prey. His ballet-like flight hypnotized the young bear as the bird soared and dropped with ease on the currents of air.

He seemed to hang motionless, and then without warning dove at its unseen prey. The air exploded in a white cloud of feathers as an unsuspecting ptarmigan was caught in mid-flight, plummeting to the ground in a death spiral.

The snow felt crisp under the cub's paws and it bounded ahead to climb a great bank to get a better view of the surrounding landscape. Suddenly, it heard a faint but approaching humming sound. It had never heard this sound before and although it sensed danger it continued toward the top of the snowbank. It placed its paw on the crest of the bank and lifted its nose to look over. A gust of wind rushed against its face and a deafening roar filled its ears. A huge creature rose up in the air, and roared with all its might. The cub turned to run and tumbled down the bank.

Dizzy from its quick decent, the cub shook its head and began again to run. The creature followed from above; its broad shadow danced ahead on the glistening snow. In a split second, the cub felt a stabbing pain in its back and fell to the ground. It tried to rise, but could not and an unfamiliar dryness filled its mouth.

The cub lay on its side, its tongue hanging lifelessly out of its mouth. It turned its eyes skyward and saw the beast directly above. Heat swept its face and made the snow dance in a circle around the cub's body. The form slowly lowered itself to the ground and settled some distance from its motionless body. Darkness was closing in. Two strange faces swam before the cub's eyes, then faded to black.

❄

That night a feast was held at the community centre. Caribou were rare near Sachs Harbour (they seldom swam across to the island) and hunters had just returned with a catch to be shared with elders and others who were not able to participate in the hunt themselves.

Napachee sat and listened as the drummers told their stories through song and dance. The drums were made from hoops of wood with animal skins stretched over their surface. When accompanied by songs in Inuvialuktun or Inuktitut the dancers moved in rhythm, telling the story of the hunt and the animals that had been captured with the movement of their bodies. Napachee watched as one of the dancers moved forward to mimic the throwing of a harpoon.

Napachee had always enjoyed listening to the stories of his grandfather and the other elders, but tonight he could not keep his mind on the songs of the hunt. The argument he had with his father kept repeating in his mind. When he tried to tell his father things about life in the South or things he learned in school, his father changed the subject. When he had asked for a computer last Christmas his father had given him a new rifle and scope. No matter what he said his father refused to listen. It was only with his mother's help that he managed to convince his father to order him more modern clothes from the South.

"What's wrong?" Napachee's mother asked now. "You are not with us tonight."

"Today I told Father I do not want to be a hunter, but he wouldn't listen. He doesn't care what *I* want; he only cares about what *he* wants!"

"Your father loves you very much, Napachee, but he is afraid of what you say. The way of the South is very different from ours and the city is not a place that has been kind to our people. Enuk wants you to be happy, but he does not know how to tell you his feelings. Be patient. Soon you will be old enough to decide for yourself what you really want, and your father will accept your decision."

"He will never understand me. Sometimes I think no one will. I see the same faces every day, nothing ever changes. I can walk from one end of town to the other in ten minutes. Father says that the land is ours and it keeps our spirits free. He is wrong! The land and the ocean around us are a trap! A trap that keeps me here and keeps me from finding where I really belong!"

Napachee slipped into silence and stared across the crowded hall. "I heard there are some white men in town from the South. Pannik saw them today. I am going to visit them tomorrow."

"Do not encourage him, Talik!"

Napachee's father had overheard their conversation and burst in angrily.

"You know nothing of the world and are not old enough to know what is right. All of this talk about computers and television and the city. If children keep leaving for the South and show no interest in our traditions soon they will all be forgotten. Your friends don't even speak their own language! They watch television instead of going hunting with their fathers, or hang around the game hall in the evenings instead of listening to the elders. What good will all this lead to? The more you go to school the more you want to move to the South. You are not to speak of these things again Napachee! Our way of life has been good enough for us for centuries and it will be good enough for you! You are not to go near the white men. Instead, you will go with me tomorrow when I go hunting." With that Enuk turned to leave.

"You are blind Father! Can't you see that our own community is getting smaller every day? One by one everyone is moving south and finding real work! The white man's ways *are* better than ours!"

"Enough!" Enuk replied angrily.

Napachee rose quickly and stormed across the crowded hall. Enuk saw the rage in Napachee's eyes and watched as he disappeared into the crowd. The angry face that he saw was his son's, but it was a son he felt he no longer knew.

"I don't know what he wants from me, Talik," Enuk said to his wife. "I look at him and I see the same boy I have always known. But I speak to him and I realize that he is only the same on the outside. No matter what I say he refuses to accept that I know what is best for him."

"He is just a boy," Talik said, "but he is a boy with

a man struggling to grow inside of him. He is confused. You have to be patient. I will go and try to talk to him," Talik said, her eyes searching the crowd for her son.

Enuk shook his head and slowly walked away.

"How can Father not understand!" Napachee blurted when she sat beside him. "Every time I want to do something or speak my own mind he refuses to accept my ideas! He treats me like a child!"

"He is just trying to do what he feels is best for you." Talik moved closer and gently placed her hand on his shoulder. Napachee pulled away and stood up suddenly. He had to get out of there!

He pushed his way across the hall, out the door and into the darkness of the night, running as fast as he could between the houses and out onto the sea ice of the harbour. He collapsed and rolled onto his back, gasping for breath. He could see the blue and green swirl of the Northern Lights high above him. As tears clouded his vision, the clouds took the shape of his father's face. The fog of his frozen breath rose into the night sky.

TWO

The polar bear cub shuddered and began to regain consciousness. It was dimly aware of unfamiliar sounds and surroundings. As it struggled to open its eyes, a terrible pain shot through its head and the bars of a cage came into focus.

James Strong had captured many animals in his long career as a zookeeper. They had surprised this polar bear cub with the helicopter and it had been an easy target for the tranquilizer gun. He was relieved to see the cub beginning to waken. It had been asleep for far too long and he had started to question whether the dose of tranquilizer they had administered had been too strong.

"There, there. You will feel sluggish for awhile but you will get better. You'll have plenty of rest on the journey ahead." James had traveled to Sachs Harbour to complete one task and one task alone. To capture two polar bear cubs and transport them to the zoo in Edmonton. He was dedicated to the preservation of wildlife and saw the zoo as a means of educating others to respect the animals and their place in nature.

The cub wobbled to its feet and peered through the bars. Gaining some confidence, it growled and shrunk to the back of the cage.

"Look at it! Once it gets its legs I'll have to teach it some discipline," Jarvis, James' assistant, muttered.

For Jarvis, animals were just part of his job; they had to be captured, broken, trained and sold. He was a bull of a man with thick arms and legs and what he lacked in height he made up for in strength and a mean disposition. He seldom shaved and had an ample belly that was barely covered by a dirty shirt. The other men feared him, but paid him grudging respect.

Jarvis slowly unlocked the cage and opened the door. The cub growled louder and braced itself against the bars.

"So, you do have some fight in you!" Jarvis sneered, picking up a short, thick stick nearby. Before James had time to intervene, Jarvis moved closer and raised the club to strike.

"Can I help look after it?" Napachee blurted, stepping out of the shadows where he'd been watching.

"Keep your distance kid," Jarvis rasped. "It's time for me to teach it who's boss!"

"Settle down Jarvis," James interrupted. "You will do no such thing!" Taking the club from Jarvis and walking toward Napachee he held out his hand by way of introduction, "My name is James and who might you be?"

"I'm Napachee. I live here, and I can look after the bear for you. I can clean it or feed it or whatever you need! I won't be any trouble and I will make sure the bear is no trouble either. I can feed it in the morning, and at lunch and in the afternoon I can clean its...."

"Slow down," James chuckled. "If it means that much to you, you can look after the bear. As long as your parents don't mind you spending the time here, I don't mind the help. Another hand or two can't hurt. I won't be able to pay you much though."

"I don't need to be paid," Napachee said eagerly, his excitement barely contained in his nervous gestures.

"Be here at 7:00 tomorrow morning. Like I said, as long as your parents agree to this it will be alright."

Napachee turned and ran for home. As he spotted his father feeding the dogs his heart sank. He would never agree to this! After their argument yesterday working for men from the South would be the last thing in the world he would allow.

Napachee barely heard his father's greeting and could only muster a weak smile as he moved past him into the house. Napachee went into his room and flopped onto his bed. He knew two things: he couldn't ask his father if he could look after the bear and he couldn't stay away from the men from the South!

❄

James had told Jarvis he didn't approve of the use of clubs and other weapons to keep animals in line and had threatened to fire him if he ever saw him attempt to beat an animal again.

Now Jarvis slowly walked towards the cage, removing the club from his pocket and stopping silently in front of the bars. The cub had curled up at the back of the cage and was sleeping peacefully. Jarvis slammed the club against the door and the cub jolted to its feet. Its eyes were slow to adjust, but it recognized the smell immediately. Baring its teeth, it growled and pressed hard against the back of the cage. Jarvis chuckled as he quietly opened the cage door and crouched in the doorway.

❆

Napachee bolted upright and wondered if he had slept too long. He lay back in his bed and began to rub the sleep from his eyes. He had spent a fitful night, tossing and turning in his sleep. Every time he had closed his eyes, he saw his father's angry face. Now he lay in the dark wondering if he really should go at all. If his father found out, he would be in big trouble. But if he didn't go he would always wonder what he had missed.

He had learned that Jarvis and James were from Edmonton and though many of his friends had been there Napachee had never had an opportunity to visit. There were other whites who lived in Sachs Harbour as well, school teachers and government employees, but most of them had been living in the North for many years and didn't often talk about their earlier life. This was his chance to hear everything first hand.

When Napachee arrived at the camp, the men were already up and working with equipment. They appeared to be packing up to leave. Napachee spotted James and headed toward him.

"Good morning. You're just in time," James said.

"Are you leaving for the South already?"

"No. We are going out with the helicopter one last time to try and get a second cub. Our contract was to capture *two* cubs for the zoo. This is our last day here, so if we don't get one today we're out of luck."

Napachee felt a rough hand on the back of his neck. Jarvis had walked up while they were talking and held a pail out to Napachee with his other hand.

"First, clean the cage. You can use this pail to wash it out and there is some clean straw over there you can spread on the bottom. Once that is done you can give it some of the food over by the tent."

"I don't think that's a good idea, Jarvis. It's not safe. We will be gone all day so you'd better feed the cub through the bars of its cage for now, and then after we get back to help you, you can clean the cage. Don't try to open the cage door while we are away. We'll see you later," James said.

With that the two men walked off leaving Napachee to the task at hand. He picked up the pail and walked over to the cage. Seeing Napachee, the cub snarled and backed up into its familiar position against the bars at the rear of the cage.

"*Qanuripit*," Napachee said, surprising himself by speaking to the cub in Inuktitut. "I won't harm you. You must be hungry. I'll get some of your food." Napachee walked to the tent and spotted the frozen fish among the provisions the men brought with them.

The young cub no longer snarled. The men had said not to open the bear cub's cage, but Napachee reached for the handle anyway. Surely it was no threat.

"There, there little one. Do not be frightened, I won't harm you." The cub did not snarl or move to the back of its cage this time. It just sat there as Napachee opened the door. It watched as Napachee filled its bowls with food and water. Napachee looked at the small cub and slowly reached out to touch its fur. He placed his hand gently upon the cub's head. The bear started to growl.

"What is this?" Napachee could feel a large bump on the side of the cub's head. He tried to inspect the wound more closely but the cub whimpered and pulled back. After a few seconds, he slowly returned his hand to the bear's head and began to feel the rest of its body. He found a series of bumps and dried blood along its left ear.

Just then his sister, Pannik, called to him. She wore an *amoute* their mother had sewn and it held Napachee's little brother in the hood on her back.

"Come on. Father is looking for you and you don't want to be late!"

"How did you find me?"

"Mother thought this might be where you had

gone and she asked me to get you right away."

Napachee hurriedly closed the cage door and set the pail down before leaving with his sister.

"I will be back later little one," Napachee shouted over his shoulder. The cub cocked its head in curiosity as they disappeared. Alone, it slumped to the floor of its cage and tenderly began to lick its wounds.

❄

The morning was a very slow one for Napachee. He worked with his father, but heard nothing that was said. Napachee was certain that Jarvis had something to do with the lumps that covered the young cub's body. Something had struck it and it had not been by accident.

"The spool! Napachee pass me the spool!" Napachee surfaced from his thoughts and passed his father the spool of string they were using to mend their fishing nets. They used the nets to catch Arctic Char. Napachee loved Char, especially when his mother took the fresh fish, froze it in layers before cutting it into small pieces and served it raw. This was called *quaq*. Caribou could be served the same way, but Napachee preferred Char *quaq*.

"Joseph has a new dog he wants me to meet. Can I go before it gets too late?" Napachee asked, feeling guilty for the lie.

His father nodded. "Don't be late for lunch!"

Enuk heard the porch door open as Talik brought

him a cup of coffee. He took the cup, gently.

"Who can figure these young ones out? It seems the more they learn the more they want what they don't have. They want to move to Inuvik, Yellowknife or the South. Will they leave their elders behind?" Talik gave him a comforting look and then Enuk returned to the the task of mending the net.

Once beyond his father's gaze, Napachee took off his fur hat and replaced it with a baseball cap. As he wandered along the road he stared out across the frozen expanse of ice. The road didn't go beyond the community itself. The only way to travel to another community was to fly, or go over the ocean and land without aid of a road. He imagined what lay on the ocean's other shore. He had been to Inuvik of course, but he had never been to Yellowknife or Edmonton. Napachee watched his feet as they crunched on the hard packed snow.

"Napachee! Come on in!"

Snapping out of his thoughts he turned to wave to Joseph calling him from the steps of the game hall.

"If I hadn't shouted at you, you would have walked right past," Joseph said.

"It's my father again," Napachee said with a sigh. "He never understands what I want. I don't think he wants to understand."

"He's kind of old fashioned, but what can you do? My father doesn't understand *me* either. I've given up."

"Joseph, *I* don't even understand you most of the time, so how can you expect your father to?"

The two friends looked at each other and started to laugh as they entered the game hall.

"I saw your father yesterday with the dogs and sled. Are you going out for the hunt again? I told *my* father I had better things to do with my time."

"Like foozeball." Napachee agreed and the two friends went to the foozeball table and started a game. Every day was the same: school, the game hall, the community centre, video games and hunting. Nothing ever changed! He liked his friends and the hockey and volleyball games they had at the centre but there had to be more.

"Yah!" Joseph said as he scored to end the game.

"I'm not concentrating very well. I can't stop thinking about the fight I had with my father."

Looking over Napachee's shoulder, Joseph put his finger to his lips to signal him to be quiet. Napachee turned and saw his father approaching.

"Let's go, Napachee," Enuk said sternly.

"But we just started to...."

"Napachee I don't have time to argue with you. The ice is perfect for sealing and I want you to come along."

Napachee opened his mouth to argue but gave up before he uttered a word. He went to the door with his father, but he turned back in time to see Joseph shake his head as he walked toward the others.

Napachee followed his father to the sled and they headed out across the harbour and away from town. The day was beautiful and despite his dark mood Napachee turned toward the sun and enjoyed the warmth on his face. It reflected brightly off of the snow and Napachee put on his sunglasses to guard against snow blindness. At least he didn't have to wear the old wooden snow glasses his grandfather had once left laying around! He could imagine the reaction he'd get from Joseph and his other friends if they saw him in those!

As they neared a patch of open water Enuk called the dogs to a halt. Jumping off, he walked to the water's edge and knelt to examine the snow. A trace of fur and markings near the water indicated that several seal had been sunbathing there not too long ago. Smiling, Enuk returned to the sled. He carefully unfastened a tarp and gently removed the harpoon Napachee's grandfather had used many years ago.

"Would you like to try today?"

Napachee shook his head and looked away. He didn't want to see his father's hurt expression.

Enuk got comfortable by the water's edge. Almost all hunters used a rifle to hunt seal, but Enuk liked to use a harpoon as his own father had. It took extreme patience to sit for hours by the water's edge waiting for a seal to emerge for air or sunshine. Napachee lay back on the sled and closed his eyes.

A half-hour passed and then a commotion roused Napachee and he sat up. His father had harpooned a seal and had, expertly and quickly, laid it on the ice.

As he knelt beside the animal, Enuk picked up a handful of snow and placed it in his mouth. Once it had melted, he opened the seal's mouth and spit the liquid snow inside. This was a tradition in the eastern arctic and showed respect. Enuk gave thanks to the animal for giving its life to sustain the lives of the hunter and his family.

Walking to the sled Enuk spoke quietly to his son, "You used to love to go hunting. You used to love to hear the stories of the spirits of the dead who have come back as animals. Remember what the elders have said about communicating with animals."

Napachee turned to speak, but decided to remain quiet. His father had captured the seal and Napachee was anxious to get back and finish his chores with the bear cub before the white men returned.

Even though Napachee said nothing, Enuk could see his son's look of disinterest. With a heavy heart he lashed his catch to the sled and turned for home.

When they reached their house, Napachee quickly changed his clothes and left for the white man's camp, a circle of tents near the airstrip only ten minutes away.

The men had not returned from their day of hunting yet. All was quiet and deserted.

Napachee slowly approached the bear's cage and stared through the bars. The cub had been napping and it jumped with fright. Napachee chuckled. The cub cocked its head to one side and listened.

Napachee heard a noise behind him and turned to see Jarvis scowling at him in disgust.

"Taking care of that cub is a man's job and if you can't be trusted to get it done like one, and fast, then you'll have to leave!"

Napachee had been so intent on his duties he had not heard the helicopter land some distance away. Despite being out all day the men had not found another bear cub. Everyone was in a bad mood, but Jarvis was especially ready to vent his anger.

Jarvis turned and walked over to the others. Napachee couldn't hear what was being said, but he could tell a decision was being made. Napachee went toward them and James stood to give instructions.

"Our cargo plane leaves early tomorrow morning, so this is the last job we have for you. I will have one of the men come over and help you clean the cage."

"That's O.K. The cub seems fine around me, was this morning too. Watch."

To prove his confidence Napachee picked up some clean straw and returned to the bear cub's cage and opened the door.

The cub was not frightened and sniffed the straw curiously. The touch of its wet nose on Napachee's cheek caused him to start and the cub jumped. Napachee rubbed the cub behind its ear with one hand and fingered the straw with the other. He had an idea.

"I will name you *Hagiyok*, 'strong one' in Inuktitut. Perhaps it will be a good omen and you will be strong enough to free us both from our cages. Now, I need more straw, some cooperation and a little luck," he whispered.

THREE

Hagiyok's eyes opened and the cub tentatively sniffed the air. Something had disturbed its sleep. Slowly it closed its eyes and turned again to its bed of straw.

A dark figure stood beside the storage shed. It crouched and then ran behind the cage and waited. The voices of the white men and the smell of cigarette smoke drifted on the cold night air.

Hagiyok awoke and stiffened as it heard the cage door open. The cub peered through the darkness and bared its teeth to growl. A hand clasped firmly over its muzzle so all it could do was squeak.

❄

Jarvis stood at the edge of the camp and took one last drag of his cigarette before flicking it into the darkness. He and the other men loaded the cage that held the bear cub onto the sled behind the snowmobile, and secured it with ropes. The cub lay quietly on the floor of its cage, nestled in the deep bed of straw that Napachee had placed there. Only the top of its head and its eyes poked out in the early morning air.

"That straw will make it more comfortable. The boy did a good job. I wonder where he got to? He said he would come and see us before we left, to say goodbye." James said, worry in his voice.

The snowmobile jerked into motion and headed off toward the airstrip. A few minutes later it had pulled up to the freight plane's cargo door and the men lifted the cage into the hold and secured it tightly with the freight straps that hung from the cargo bay wall.

Jarvis tugged on the straps to make sure they were secure and slapped his club loudly on the top of the cage.

The cub shivered as the freight door closed with a hollow bang. The plane throbbed to life and the cargo hold began to shake. The straw at the cub's feet rustled, and Napachee stuck his head out from a patch of straw near the paws of the young bear.

"We are flying Hagiyok! We are on our way!"

❊

Napachee had only flown once before when his family had moved from Cambridge Bay to Sachs Harbour and the flight had not been anything like this! The cargo hold was dark and very cold. He had not eaten since the previous day and his stomach ached with hunger. But when they hit turbulence the hunger no longer mattered. He was too sick to even think about eating anything!

The whole trip terrified Hagiyok so that the bear huddled in a corner with its nose tucked under its paw. The cub watched as Napachee sat curled up in a ball, moaning and holding his stomach. Napachee kept his eyes closed and tried to think of good things to keep his mind off of his stomach and his future.

❋

After some time Napachee sensed a change in the sound of the airplane. He could feel the pressure changing in his ears and knew they had started their decent. This new excitement made him forget his discomfort and he nestled back into the straw and waited for the plane to land.

They soon touched down and taxied to a stop. Napachee could hear voices outside and the cargo door open, bringing a welcome gust of fresh air into the hold. People moved around the hold but after a few minutes they left again and all became quiet as the door to the hold was closed. In a few moments the plane began to move again, gaining speed as it raced along the runway for takeoff.

They must have touched down in Inuvik for gas before continuing further south. To Napachee's relief the trip was now much smoother and he settled into a restful sleep. The cub was drowsy from the altitude and dozed off and on for the remainder of the trip.

ROBERT FEAGAN

Napachee awoke again when his ears began to pop. He had no idea how long he had been resting. The plane seemed to be losing altitude, the engines had a different pitch and changed direction.

They touched down in what he could only guess was Yellowknife. Runways in the cities were paved! Once again the door opened and men hoisted themselves into the cargo bay. A flurry of conversation reached Napachee's ears.

From what Napachee could hear the men were now negotiating a flat-bed truck rental to transport the cub for the remaining day trip to Edmonton. This would be quicker than waiting for the next cargo plane as the one they were in concluded its run in Yellowknife and it would be easier on the bear.

An hour later, Napachee felt the cage being lifted off the plane and put onto the truck. After much effort and commotion, the final leg of their trip began. Napachee tried to see the countryside as it passed by, but from his vantage point in the straw he only caught bits and pieces of the scenery. His legs were cramped and beginning to fall asleep. He remained still for as long as he could but finally he couldn't manage the discomfort any further. He pushed himself up and gathered his legs beneath him, slowly poking his head out of the straw. He could see Jarvis and another man deep in conversation in the cab of the truck.

He reached up and gripped the top of the cage. Being careful not to raise much above the level of the straw, Napachee straightened his legs. He closed his eyes and took a deep breath of fresh air and feeling began to return to the lower portion of his body. He dared to look ahead into the cab of the truck for only a second, but in that moment he saw Jarvis in the rearview mirror looking back at him!

Jarvis jerked his head around and opened his mouth in shock. The truck swerved across the centreline of the road and into the path of an oncoming car. Jarvis jerked it back to avoid a collision, but overcompensated so that the vehicle hit the soft shoulder and the steering became sluggish. He fought to bring the truck back onto the road, but it began to skid out of control. The truck turned sideways and then flipped onto its side.

The metal frame screamed against the pavement sending a shower of sparks high in the air as the truck smashed to a jarring halt against a telephone pole. The impact threw the cage off of the back and it slid to the edge of the trees that lined the highway.

When the young cub opened its eyes, it could see that the cage door was open. It could feel Napachee squirming behind and bounded out of the cage.

Knowing he had to fend for himself or face Jarvis' wrath, Napachee turned to run as well, but stumbled on the latch as he was trying to disentangle himself from the cage. He could see the cub disappearing into the bush as he struggled to his feet.

A rough hand clamped Napachee's shoulder and threw him to the ground. He felt hot breath on the back of his neck.

"Stay where you are. I don't tolerate stowaways," threatened Jarvis.

❄

The bear cub did not stop running nor did it look back. It stood tired and panting in a small clearing in the woods. It had never been among trees before and they towered above, closing in. Desperately it charged from the clearing and began to run once more, bursting through a dense section of undergrowth at the top of a steep ridge. The cub lost its footing and tumbled down the other side, covering the distance from top to bottom in a dizzying flurry that left it gasping for breath in a pile of dry leaves.

The cub rose to its feet and shakily gathered its bearings. Looking to the edge of a stand of trees, the cub froze. Standing, looking into its eyes, was a very large brown animal, larger than a caribou, with huge fuzzy antlers.

The two animals surveyed each other. Before the cub could move the moose turned and bolted into the trees. The cub looked back up the bank in one direction and then turned its head toward the form of the moose slipping behind the trees in the other. Hagiyok followed *Itsé* the moose at a safe distance, hoping it would lead the cub home.

NAPACHEE

❄

Napachee gazed out over the city. The ride in the truck to Edmonton with Jarvis had been a long and painful one. Jarvis had kept Napachee locked in the empty bear cage until help had arrived and the trip had taken most of the endless day.

When they got to Edmonton Jarvis delivered him to James Strong at the parking lot with his parting words, "Good riddance."

Now he stood on the 20th floor of James' apartment gazing over more lights than he had ever seen in his life. He could hear the swoosh of traffic below and was amazed at how small the cars looked as they sped onward to their destinations. He watched the flashing landing lights of a small plane as it flew over the city, appearing to move in slow motion. A warm current of air blew up from the street and felt thick in Napachee's throat.

James stepped out of the apartment onto the balcony. The two stood in silence for a moment, both looking across the expanse of lights.

"I called your parents. They were worried sick when you went missing. I assured them you were alright, but your father wants to talk to you in the morning, after you're rested."

Napachee knew what his father would think of all this and he didn't want to talk to him yet.

James led Napachee back into the apartment. "You can sleep on the couch for tonight and in the morning I will try to find a cot. You and Jo can take turns between the bed and cot until you head home."

"Jo? I thought you said that you had a daughter?" Napachee said, puzzled.

James smiled. "It's short for Josephine. Don't tell her I told you that. She hates her name. Ever since her mother died five years ago she has insisted on being called Jo. She's such a tomboy that it really suits her better anyway."

James handed Napachee some blankets and motioned to the couch. "Try to get some sleep. I'll see you in the morning before I head off to work. Jo is going to keep you occupied tomorrow so you will need all the rest you can get!" James smiled and headed off to the bedroom at the end of the hall.

Napachee spread out the blankets and lay back on the couch, listening to the sounds of James getting ready for bed. Soon silence fell over the apartment. Napachee sat on the edge of the couch, rose to his feet and silently padded to the sliding doors that opened to the balcony. He quietly slid the doors open, surprised to discover how loud the sounds of the city were as they drifted up from the street below.

It was well after midnight, but nothing had stopped. The miniature world below him continued with no sign of slowing. Back home the occasional howl of a dog or roar of a snowmobile, as someone headed home from visiting a neighbor, would be the only sounds to break the silence at this hour. Napachee smiled and lifted his face skyward to take a deep contented breath. Tomorrow he would explore the world below.

Napachee walked back inside and closed the noise of the city out as he slid the balcony doors shut behind him. He returned to the couch and lay on his back with his hands resting under his head and stared at the ceiling. If only Pannik could see him now!

Napachee smiled and closed his eyes. The fatigue of the last twenty-four hours overtook his body and he eased into a deep and peaceful slumber. His dreams flowed freely and he drifted across the night's sky high above the city. Amid large trees shrouded in an early morning mist Napachee stared at a shadow beginning to take shape. A four-legged creature emerged from the fog with large fuzzy antlers, a bulbous nose and mouth and bulging eyes. It grew larger as it came closer and closer.

FOUR

Napachee awoke to the sound of voices hurried in conversation. It took him a moment to realize where he was, but he soon recalled the events of the previous day. He recognized the voices as those of James Strong and Jarvis. He closed his eyes and listened while the men continued to talk. He could tell by Jarvis' tone that he was very upset and he was sure that it had something to do with him.

"Listen Jarvis. It's not *all* the boy's fault. Now we just have to make the best of things and regroup," James said.

"But the boy...."

"Jarvis, lower your voice. Jo is still asleep and I don't want Napachee to hear all your ranting first thing in the morning!"

"Don't worry, Dad, I'm already awake."

The two men turned as James' teenaged daughter entered the room. Her striking red hair, pale white skin and multitude of freckles made her the very image of all the things James had loved about his wife.

She stopped and stared at the boy who appeared to be asleep on the couch.

"As I was saying, James, the kid almost killed us all. It was his fault we lost the cub. I'll need to go after it as soon as possible or it will die in the woodlands and our whole trip will have been a waste. It isn't worth anything to anyone if it's dead."

"He looks Japanese!" James turned from Jarvis and looked at his daughter. She had been standing staring at Napachee as he feigned sleep on the couch.

"Are you sure he is an Eskimo?"

"He is Inuvialuit, Jo, and he is definitely not from Japan. I want him to feel at home, so don't go making any comments like that once he is awake."

"I thought people from the North were called Inuit?"

"Well, some people are. Napachee comes from Sachs Harbor, which is in the western arctic, part of the Northwest Territories. People who live in that part of the North are called Inuvialuit. People who live further to the east of Holman and far across to Iqaluit are called Inuit. That territory is called Nunavut. Both peoples used to be called Eskimo, but prefer the other proper names. Eskimo means 'eaters of raw meat' and is often seen as negative. Their proper names mean 'The People'.

"I spoke to Napachee's father last night and Sachs Harbour is fogged in. The whole area, Tuktoyaktuk, and Paulatuk too, are experiencing the same thing. It's expected to last a few days. Jo and I might as well make the boy feel at home and show him Edmonton in the meantime."

Jarvis rolled his eyes and walked to the door.

"Heavy rain is hitting the area where the bear cub disappeared too, so I want you to stay put until I tell you to go looking," James said. Jarvis shrugged and slammed the door as he left.

Both James and Jo winced. They turned to check the couch and saw Napachee, now wide awake, resting on one elbow.

"I'm glad to see you're wide awake. Get dressed and I'll get you some breakfast. How about ham and eggs?"

"Do you have any cereal?" Napachee asked.

James smiled, "I guess kids are the same everywhere." He sighed as he retrieved the cereal from the cupboard.

"Milk's in the fridge, help yourself. I have to get ready to head to the zoo. We will call your parents before I leave."

As he sat eating his breakfast, Napachee couldn't help but worry about speaking to his father. Enuk would never understand why he had made this trip. His father's solemn disapproval would be far worse than any outburst of anger.

James re-entered the kitchen, picked up the phone and began dialing. When it started to connect he handed Napachee the phone and finished preparing for work.

Napachee listened as the line clicked and

sputtered, trying to finish the connection to Sachs Harbour. At the first ring Napachee's heart skipped a beat and he held his breath.

"Hello?"

His father.

"Hello?"

Napachee hesitated and then hung up the phone. "No answer," he said as James glanced up at the sound of the phone being replaced in its cradle.

"Well, don't worry. I'm sure we'll reach them later. I've got to get going now, but feel free to keep trying until you get through. I told Jo she could take the day off from school to show you around and keep you occupied. Due to the fog, it looks like you will be here for about a week before we can get a flight back to your parents. Tell Jo there is some money on the counter to keep you going for the day and I will see you tonight."

James hurried from the apartment leaving him alone in the kitchen.

Napachee finished his breakfast and returned to the couch in the living room.

"I've never seen an Inuvialouette before," Jo said as she entered the room.

"It's Inuvialuit and I'm actually both Inuvialuit and Inuit. Anyway, I've never seen someone with so many freckles and a carrot top before," Napachee replied.

Jo blushed, but controlled her temper.

"My dad says that I have to show you around for the next few days so I guess we'd better get along. My name is Jo, by the way." Despite her attempts not to,

Jo smiled and headed into the kitchen.

"I'll go ahead and meet you downstairs," Jo shouted over her shoulder as she headed to the door. "I don't think you will want to wear your parka, so put on one of my dad's windbreakers in the front closet."

After gathering a wallet and a map that James had left for him, Napachee hurriedly got dressed and grabbed the jacket on the way out of the apartment.

Despite the fact that Jarvis had kept him in close check en route to Edmonton, Napachee had fallen asleep for the last portion of the long trip and when he got to the apartment he was in such a drowsy stupor he couldn't even remember how he had arrived on the 20th floor.

Now, the hall looked unfamiliar to him. He walked from one end to the other. There was no way out! None of the doors opened and he could not see stairs anywhere. As he walked along the hall once again, he heard a faint bell, and a large, sliding door opened.

"You headed down?" The man who asked him was standing in a small room with no windows or other doors. "I don't have all day so if you are headed down you'd better hop in now!"

An elevator. Of course! The doors started to close and Napachee jumped in. The floor started to vibrate and Napachee had the same feeling in his stomach that he had experienced in the plane. He wanted to get out, but closed his eyes and held his breath instead. Eventually, the elevator stopped shaking and the doors opened.

Napachee opened his eyes and saw three strangers staring at him, waiting to get in. He walked past them and out into the lobby on the ground floor. Jo wasn't anywhere to be seen.

He stepped out of the front door and was almost bowled over by a man in a black suit and tie. The man stumbled and looked back angrily at Napachee as he hurried off. The daylight was bright and extremely hot. Napachee removed the jacket and stood in the middle of the sidewalk for a moment while his eyes adjusted.

People were pushing past him on either side and he began to panic as he was jostled about. He instinctively backed away from the middle of the sidewalk and pressed himself against the side of the building. All the faces that passed looked unfriendly and the people that bumped into him looked at him as if it was his fault.

"What are you doing over there?" Jo asked, walking toward him from the door of the apartment building.

"Where were you?" Napachee blurted, his voice full of anger.

"What are you so upset about? I was just checking the mail, it took a minute to find you."

Napachee could feel himself beginning to blush and quickly turned away.

"Come on. If we don't hurry we will miss the bus!"

Jo moved ahead into the crowd and Napachee broke into a run to follow her. He caught a glimpse of her now and then as she threaded her way along the crowded sidewalk while he rushed on ignoring the angry shouts of people he bumped into.

Despite his efforts Napachee lost sight of Jo in a few minutes and stopped, panting at a busy corner. As he bent over to catch his breath he looked helplessly along the street in both directions.

"Hey Napachee!"

At the sound of Jo's voice Napachee looked up quickly and spotted her on the other side of the street. He took a step into the street and quickly jumped back when a car beeped its horn loudly and raced past. He waited for the light to change and started across the street with a crowd of others. A bus pulled up and Jo shouted for him to hurry as she climbed on. Napachee lunged for the bus door and squeezed inside just as it closed behind him.

"Exact change," the driver said in a low voice without looking in his direction. When Napachee didn't respond or drop any money into the receptacle, the driver gave him an angry glance.

"If you don't have the money you're off at the next stop," the bus driver said gruffly.

Jo dropped a handful of change into the slot. She led Napachee to the back of the bus and grabbed an overhead bar.

Napachee stood in silence as the bus began to move ahead. He looked around at all of the unfamiliar faces. The bus was very full and he stood wedged between two other passengers. The closeness made him uncomfortable. He took a deep breath. The bus passed several theatres with the latest movies, some comic book stores and a McDonald's. Napachee smiled to himself and started to relax. This was the city!

"Here is our stop!" Jo exclaimed as she walked to the front of the bus.

"Come on," she shouted.

"Where are we going now?" Napachee asked, trying desperately to keep up.

"We need to catch the subway!" she yelled.

Napachee followed her as she disappeared down a long flight of stairs. They turned a corner and more stairs lay before them. Once at the bottom, they reached a platform and stood waiting for the subway.

"Why do we have to catch a subway?" Napachee asked, somewhat confused.

"Edmonton is a big place. The zoo where Dad works isn't just around the corner. If you want to go somewhere you have to plan for it and it takes some time to get there. It's actually not that bad. We should be there in about twenty minutes."

Napachee shook his head. People must spend half their lives going places instead of actually being there!

After the subway and another short bus ride they arrived at the zoo.

James showed them around and gave them a tour of most of the pavilions. Napachee couldn't believe how small the cages were. The animals didn't have much room to move and most seemed to be either asleep or lying on the floor. Many were from other parts of the world, breeds he had never seen before.

He was especially impressed by the cheetah! He had learned in school about its amazing speed and beauty. He wondered how it felt, trapped here and unable to use the speed it possessed.

After their tour, James took Napachee and Jo to a nearby park where they ate lunch at a picnic table.

"I brought along some hot dogs as well as some sandwiches, but I forgot to bring wood for the fire!"

Napachee smiled and ran over to a cluster of trees. Before Jo or her father could speak, Napachee had his knife out and began chopping at some of the smaller branches of a dead tree for kindling to start a fire.

"Don't touch that! You can't just cut trees down and gather wood wherever you want," James said.

"Then how do you start a fire?" Napachee asked.

"If you want to start a fire in the park you have to get a permit. If you need wood you either buy it and bring it with you or you have to buy it from one of the attendants that work here."

Napachee was dismayed, but reluctantly agreed to play by their rules. They returned to the picnic table and finished their lunch.

The subway and bus rides back to the apartment didn't seem as long on the way home. For supper that night James ordered Chinese food and they watched TV well into the evening.

FIVE

The next day Napachee and Jo went to the West Edmonton mall. They passed dozens of restaurants, a skating rink, a huge marina with dolphins and a submarine that took people under the water for a tour. There was also a swimming pool with water slides and a wave machine! Napachee stood in wonder as the man-made waves rose up like those he had seen on the ocean. Napachee was sure that the mall was at least three times the size of Sachs Harbour itself!

Napachee stared in disbelief, his neck constantly craned to one side or the other. He ran smack into a man rushing past, his kids in tow. The force of their collision knocked Napachee off his feet and he fell hard into the lap of an elderly lady sitting on a bench.

"Watch where you're going!" the man shouted over his shoulder without slowing his pace.

"I'm sorry," Napachee said weakly under his breath, looking first at the man and then the lady glaring at him as he removed himself from her lap. Napachee could feel himself starting to sweat. He suddenly realized how many people were packed into this indoor world.

"The crowds starting to get to you?" Jo laughed.

"The mall is so enormous yet somehow all of these people still make it feel very small!"

"We need to pick up the pace or we're going to be late meeting my friends. We're late already!"

Napachee followed Jo, staying right behind her as she broke a path through the crowd. When they finally reached the arcade, and Jo's friends, Jo introduced them to Napachee. No one seemed too impressed.

"So, where are you from anyway?" Jill asked.

"He comes from the Northwest Territories," Jo answered before Napachee could even open his mouth to speak. "From a place called Sachs Harbour, you know, the arctic."

"The arctic! What is there to do up there besides hunt?" Tammy asked.

Tim added, with an angry look on his face, "It should be illegal. Most of the animals they kill are near extinction!"

"Many people who don't know the North believe what you've said. But it isn't true! None of the animals that the people in the Northwest Territories or Nunavut hunt are near extinction. My people and the other peoples of the arctic have lived in harmony with, and have respect for, the animals of the land. Hunting and trapping has been a way of life for many years and has been an important source of income and survival.

"Our people do not kill more animals than they need and use traps that are very humane so that the animals do not suffer. And yet people who do not know better protest, criticizing those that wear the coats made from our furs. Do you know what that has done? It has caused great hardship for many families who relied on hunting and trapping to live and eat. Without a demand for furs many have been forced to rely on welfare to live. They have not only lost their pride but also their independence.

"I know it isn't your fault but without thinking about how you affect the lives of my people, you and others like you protest against hunting, trapping and the fur trade in the North. You should learn the facts before you condemn us."

"O.K. O.K. Take it easy. I guess there's more to it than I had thought," said Tim.

"All that sounds pretty serious, but what about the fun stuff. Do you still live in igloos?" Jill laughed.

"No," Napachee smiled. "The population of Sachs Harbour is only two hundred and fifty and there are no other communities for hundreds of miles. But we do have television and several of the other things you would expect to see in a house here. Most differences are the result of our harsh climate. There are no trees in Sachs Harbour so the wind can get very strong. The roofs of our houses are covered in metal because shingles blow off. And there is permafrost very close to the surface of the ground in the arctic so we can't bury pipes to bring and take water away from our houses. We have two holding tanks attached to the house, filled by trucks that pump the water in and out. With this system we get running water just like you do; we just have to be careful how fast we use our water or we'll run out before the next truck comes to fill up the tank."

"It's funny people still think of igloos when they think of the arctic," Jo said.

Napachee nodded. "I can understand that," he said. "It really wasn't that long ago that people still lived on the land. My parents were both born in tents out on the tundra. It wasn't until the 1960s that aboriginal people in the arctic started to live in communities. Before that we were very nomadic and moved when we had to for food and shelter."

"Are there cars in Sachs Harbour?" asked Tim.

"The roads are all gravel there so we have trucks and four-wheelers," replied Napachee. "There really isn't anywhere to drive because the road ends just outside the community. We use four-wheelers, snowmobiles and boats to get out on the land and we have a gravel airstrip where planes can land.

"In summer, barges come in from the ocean and bring us supplies for the winter. Our vegetables and other fresh foods are brought in by plane every week. Because the fresh food is flown in it is very expensive. Sometimes we pay as much as six dollars for two litres of milk."

"We only pay two dollars here!" Tim gasped.

"Does it really stay dark night *and* day in the winter?" Tammy asked.

"In the dead of winter it stays dark all day. Then in summer we get twenty-four hours of daylight. Our summers are very short so we make the most of them and get out on the land as much as possible. The tundra is beautiful in the summer: every type of wild flower, fox, hare, ptarmigan, weasels, lemmings!"

"Don't you get depressed and sleepy in all that darkness?" Jo asked.

"Actually it's not too bad," Napachee replied. "We still go hunting in the winter and we camp in tents with heaters, or in my father's case, igloos."

"That's so cool!" Tim exclaimed.

"We cut blocks out of the hard, wind-packed snow to make the igloos. Not many people still do it, but my father is one of them. It's actually kind of fun."

Napachee paused, surprised by his enthusiasm for a place he was so desperate to leave.

The rest of the afternoon was spent going on rides, playing pool and eating junk food. As they rode the bus home that evening, Napachee sat quietly looking out the window. He had eaten at McDonald's three times, but the thrill was over; he longed for food from the land. Nothing was turning out the way he had planned. The city was so different than what he had imagined. Everything was far away and everyone was in such a rush to get there. How could he be surrounded by so many people and still feel so lonely?

After supper that night, Napachee felt the need to

get away by himself. He told Jo and James that he was just going around the block, and promised to be back in half and hour. Once out on the street, he walked along in silence.

Napachee was quiet, but his surroundings were not. There were not as many people this time of night, but the cars and traffic continued. Even here he couldn't get away and really be alone. Napachee jumped as a man stepped forward from the shadows and asked him for change. Napachee had never seen someone beg before, and though a little taken aback he did offer him what he had and continued on.

In Sachs Harbor if Napachee needed to be by himself, he jumped on his snowmobile and could be out in the middle of tundra, miles away from anyone, within minutes. Here there was no escape!

When he returned to the apartment, James passed on news from his father. "It looks like you may have to stay here longer than we thought. On top of the bad weather there is a problem with the tickets."

A few hours ago those words would have made Napachee's heart sing, but now it made it ache!

❄

Napachee opened his eyes and waited for them to slowly adjust to the dim light of the living room. He strained to see the clock on the back of the stove in the kitchen from where he lay. Three thirty a.m.

He slipped from beneath the blankets on the

couch and quickly padded across the floor to the linen closet in the hall. He had remained fully clothed when he went to bed last night so he wouldn't have to fumble around to dress in the dark.

He opened the closet for his knapsack: matches, candles, string, a hunting knife and other items he'd need on the trek. He reached further into the closet and removed his warmer northern clothing. Without turning on the light, he used two strands of his rope to tie some blankets to the knapsack.

Napachee crept back to the kitchen and put the note he had written to James on the kitchen table. He walked to the door, placed his hand on the knob and slowly started to turn it.

"Where do you think you're going!"

Napachee jumped back and bumped into Jo.

"What are you doing sneaking up on me like that!"

"What are you doing trying to sneak out of the apartment at this hour?"

Napachee turned away from Jo and stared at the door in the darkness.

"I know where you are going and I want to go with you. You didn't think I noticed, but I saw you hiding things away after supper last night. You're planning on going home."

"I heard your father talking to Jarvis last night. The rains have stopped so Jarvis is driving to the spot where the bear cub ran away to try and track it down. They are leaving this morning and I want to go with them. They are taking your father's van."

"And just how were you going to get into the van without being noticed?" Jo asked with a smile.

"Well, I hadn't really figured that out," Napachee answered timidly.

Still smiling, Jo held out her hand and dangled a key in Napachee's face. "You see you do need me. I just happen to have the spare key! I also thought these sleeping bags might come in handy and they would be warmer than a couple of old blankets."

Jo couldn't be dissuaded so she grabbed *her* knapsack and the two of them went to the underground parking and hid themselves behind a huge tool box in the back of the van. They settled in to wait but, given the hour, they soon dozed off.

A few hours later Napachee heard voices beside the van. He recognized Jarvis right away. He elbowed Jo hard in the stomach and she bolted upright. He quickly pushed her head back down and out of sight and held his breath.

The back door of the van opened and Jarvis and another man tossed some things in, closed the door, jumped into the driver's and passenger's seats and started the engine. The van started to move. After some time the men began to speak loudly enough that Napachee and Jo could overhear most of what they were saying.

"If we can pick up any trail of that cub, Timmons, then we can start a full scale hunt tomorrow. That land isn't meant for a polar bear though, so it won't surprise me if it is dead already," Jarvis wheezed.

Napachee remembered Timmons from Sachs Harbour. With pallid skin and sunken cheeks, Timmons stood about six feet tall and looked like he only weighed a hundred pounds. He nodded and didn't say much for the rest of the ride.

The ride was long and the conditions were cramped. Jarvis made good time but the drive still took more than a day. The trip was punctuated by broken sleep, stale air, heat and the growing need to use the washroom. By the time they finally arrived both Napachee and Jo were desperate! They soon heard welcome words from Jarvis.

"Here it is, Timmons. Pull over to the side. We should be able to track it from here easily."

The two men jumped out of the van and came around to the back to retrieve their guns and backpacks before heading off into the woods. Napachee and Jo had gone unseen.

Once they were sure Jarvis was out of range, Napachee opened the door and burst out of the van. They took a few moments to get the feeling back into their legs and regain their bearings. Motioning for Jo to follow, Napachee crept to the edge of the woods and watched the men move through the growth.

After some time, the men stopped and knelt to examine the ground. They had done this several times, but this time they seemed more interested. Finally the men stood up and moved along the bottom of the ridge they had been following.

Napachee and Jo moved ahead and looked down

at the spot where the men had lingered. There were the bear cub's tracks, clearly outlined in the mud! But beside them were much larger tracks.

"Those are moose tracks," Jo whispered. She recognized the tracks from various camping trips with her father, but Napachee had never seen anything bigger than caribou or deer tracks.

Napachee and Jo continued to follow the men through the woods, being careful to stay well back and out of sight. The forest floor felt cool and fresh and after some time, the men came to a small river. They crossed to the other side and seemed to falter, looking for fresh tracks, but turning in circles.

They could hear Jarvis swearing loudly across the river. Finally they headed off into the bushes on the other side, but they seemed less sure of where they were going.

Napachee and Jo crossed the river and looked at the ground. Something was wrong.

The large tracks were here, but seemed several days old. The tracks *leading* to the spot, however, had been fresh. Napachee retraced their steps to the edge of the river and began to cross back over.

"I'm trying to follow you so I hope you know what you're doing," Jo said with determination.

Napachee nodded and continued to cross until he was back on the other bank of the river. He headed downstream with Jo tagging behind him, and kept his eyes to the ground.

There! Coming out of the water were the tracks of

the moose and the polar bear cub. They were fresh! They followed them for several hours, crossing areas where the tracks were faint, or where there were odd broken branches or crushed undergrowth. Napachee looked at the sun as it dipped low over the horizon.

"Let's stop here for the night. We're in a sheltered spot and we can get an early start in the morning."

Jo nodded as she slipped her pack off and placed it on the ground.

"Napachee I can't figure this out," Jo said. "The tracks of the moose and the polar bear cut so close to each other. Are they traveling together?"

"I don't think so. It looks to me like the cub has been *following* the moose. If it spotted a moose it wouldn't know what else to do but to follow it."

Napachee walked to the river's edge and as he drank the cool water his body began to feel refreshed. They had only eaten a few crackers, some cheese and an apple they brought with them since they left the apartment and the hunger pangs were getting stronger. They had wanted to keep their packs light and Jo's father hadn't had many portable dry goods on hand the night they left.

Napachee selected a young tree and broke it free. He took out the hunting knife and began to slice at the bark until the end was fashioned into a point. Dinner wouldn't be hard to find.

SIX

Napachee rose early the next morning and went to work. The water of the river was cold and clear. They had to eat soon to keep their energy up and he had seen trout last night before he went to sleep. Napachee chose a turn in the river where the water was forced into a shallow pool. He took rocks from along the edge and built a funnel shaped channel leading from the faster water into the slower current of the pool. Inuit had trapped fish in this manner many years ago and his father had shown him how to do it when he was very young in Cambridge Bay. The fish would swim into the funnel and get trapped in the pool of water. They could then be speared by a patient hunter.

He watched intently as the first fish swam into his man-made channel and stopped to rest in the pool. In a few minutes there were four big fish resting in the shallows. Napachee held his spear high and threw.

When Jo awoke she could smell something good

cooking on a fire. She peered out from the lean-to she had built the night before, propped herself on one elbow in her sleeping bag to see Napachee carefully tending a fire. Napachee slept in his sleeping bag under the stars. He had not brought a tent with him, preferring the crisp outdoor air.

Seeing her movement out of the corner of his eye, Napachee turned and smiled. "Breakfast is served."

❄

The next two days were hot and the two friends stopped frequently for water and rest. The nearly twenty-four hours of daylight had begun to shorten, but the weather was still extremely warm and dry. Napachee and Jo took advantage of the many lakes and streams that dotted the landscape to keep cool and to supply them with a continual source of fresh water. They kept a good supply of fish as well and were not hungry during their hours of walking.

It was late in the season so the mosquitoes had started to die off, but black flies were out in full force.

"Aaaaaaaah!" Jo shouted in frustration. "I'm going to go insane if they don't stop biting me!" she cried in exasperation as she swatted behind her ears.

"We should be better off tomorrow. The mosquitoes and black flies are attracted to shampoo, deodorant and perfumes. Once we wash a few more times most of it will wear off and they won't be as attracted to us. We could cover ourselves in mud as well, if you think it will help."

"Don't you *know* if it works?"

"Not really. In Sachs Harbour there are no trees and bushes. We don't really get many mosquitoes and black flies. Just try to keep your mind off of them for now. We are catching up to Hagiyok. The tracks are much fresher here."

❇

As the day passed, the land began to get rougher and more hilly. Dusk approached and the cub stopped for a drink of water at a small stream. It had followed the moose until it had the confidence to travel on its own. This land was still unfamiliar, but the fear that had first gripped the cub had now subsided. It lifted its head and sniffed the air. The cub had an uneasy feeling. It crossed the stream and began to walk faster up a hill. It looked back and began to run, sure it could see shadows moving behind it.

As it neared the top, a wolf leapt in front of the cub. Two more approached from the side, and one from the rear. Wolves would not normally attack a polar bear, but this was a cub, and one weakened by lack of food. The biggest wolf bared its teeth and emitted a low menacing growl.

The bear made a feeble attempt at a growl of its own and struck out at its tormentors.

Another wolf bared its teeth as it stepped forward and moved toward the cub. It circled behind and the cub turned, trying to face the enemy.

The wolf slunk slowly to the left and then right. All at once it lunged and leapt toward the cub!

At that moment a spear pierced the wolf's shoulder, driving it backwards and pinning it to the ground. It cried with pain, and tried to struggle free as the pack scattered madly in all directions.

Napachee raced to the cub as wolves ran howling into the bushes. After ensuring the cub was unharmed, Napachee rose and slowly walked toward the wolf, still pinned in place by the spear. He stood above it and stared into its eyes. The wolf began to snarl, then lowered its eyes and lay still.

Napachee pulled the spear from the wolf, freeing it from the ground. Its head remained lowered while it cautiously moved off toward the bushes. It neared the edge of cover and leapt ahead, running into the darkness that the dense growth provided. The sounds of the wolf's rapid retreat and its frequent whimpers of pain faded away and the clearing fell into silence.

Napachee turned to the polar bear cub and motioned for Jo to approach from where she had been standing downhill. He walked over to his belongings and pulled out some fish he had speared earlier. He held the fish out to the cub.

"Eat, Hagiyok. You must be hungry."

The cub was unsure, but at the sound of the boy's voice, it cocked his head to the side and listened intently. It had not forgotten the boy or his kindness and any hesitation it might have felt disappeared as the smell of fresh fish reached its nostrils. The cub moved toward Napachee and stretched forward to take the fish from his hand. It stopped short, looking Napachee in the eye, and calmly licked his hand. Taking the fish in its mouth, Hagiyok moved away from Napachee and settled into the first meal it had eaten in days.

Jo watched, amazed. "The bear is so comfortable with you. I thought it would be wild!"

"It is a young cub and had not yet learned to hunt from its mother before it was separated. It seems to remember me and will likely follow us to camp with the promise of more food."

"Do you think we should find a sheltered spot for the night?"

"Yes, let's move to the top of this hill and scout out a good spot before we lose the light."

Picking up their things the two friends continued up the hill with the polar bear cub in close pursuit. As they had hoped there was a small valley just on the other side that offered protection from the wind and a perfect spot to set up and build a fire.

After eating fish and berries found along their trail, Napachee and Jo climbed into their sleeping bags and drifted off to sleep. Napachee dreamt he was swirling and floating over mountains and into the clouds. The world became dark and a fire glowed in the distance. As he neared the fire he could see people huddled around it telling stories. He sat among them with Hagiyok and Jo and waited for direction.

❊

Napachee felt something brush his ear. He was just enjoying his first good night's sleep in days and he did not want to open his eyes. He snuggled deeper beneath his sleeping bag and tried to push the light and thoughts from his mind. But he heard a rattling sound close by and slowly opened his eyes.

There, only a few feet away, was one of the largest ravens he had ever seen. It was intently digging into his pack and pulling everything that wasn't tied down out into the clearing. Napachee lifted his head and opened his mouth to shout. Before he could make a sound the raven fluttered backwards and settled near the sleeping form of Jo.

Flashing his bright, beady eyes at Napachee, *Tasó* the raven began looking around for something to disturb. With nothing else close at hand it began to pick and tug at Jo's sleeping bag. With each tug the bag slipped lower and lower on Jo's sleeping form until she lay shivering in her clothes.

With a start she sat up, and through bleary eyes began to blink against the morning light. She looked first at Napachee who was now laughing and then at the raven who had hopped to the other side of the camp. Still unsure of what had happened, but feeling she was somehow the brunt of a joke, Jo's face reddened with anger.

"It's only a raven."

Jo looked at Napachee and then back across at

the raven. It had now located a half-eaten fish that Hagiyok had left before falling asleep, and was noisily crunching it, bones and all.

Napachee and Jo watched as Hagiyok started to twitch and rouse from sleep at the noisy sounds of the meal being eaten close by. The cub opened its eyes and without moving watched as the brazen bird consumed the fish only feet away.

Then, without warning, Hagiyok tensed, and sprang at the raven with all of its might. The raven calmly fluttered up just out of the cub's reach and landed on the lowest branch of a nearby tree. Napachee and Jo laughed as Hagiyok sat beneath the tree in puzzled frustration.

"Ravens are one of the smartest birds in the world," Napachee explained. "They are capable of things most people would never imagine. They will pick the lids off of garbage cans and then throw everything out just to get the scraps they want to eat. Most people in the North build wooden containers to put their garbage in just so the ravens can't make a mess. Ravens also tease dogs and other animals with their noise and antics."

Jo smiled and shook her head as she stared up at the beady-eyed pirate who looked down on the camp.

Napachee walked over to Hagiyok and gave the cub a scratch behind the ear. "Come here Jo. I want to introduce you two."

Jo tentatively walked over to where Napachee crouched by Hagiyok and knelt down beside them.

Hagiyok looked at Jo questioningly and shifted closer to Napachee.

"Hagiyok this is my friend Jo. She is going to make our journey with us."

Jo looked proudly at Napachee and held her hand out to the cub. Hagiyok sniffed Jo's hand with little interest and rubbed its head against Napachee. Napachee could see the disappointment on Jo's face.

"It will take a while Jo. Hagiyok has been through a lot. I'm surprised it is being this friendly to *me*. Give it a few days. Let's eat some fish for breakfast and then continue on our way."

Napachee left Jo and the young bear and went about preparing breakfast.

"Why are you doing this Napachee?" Jo asked a few moments later. "I know the city didn't end up being what you expected, but why go home the hard way? If you had waited another few days you could have gone home by plane and you know your father would have been happy to see you."

Napachee stopped what he was doing and turned to Jo. "What would that have proven? What would I do? Get off the plane and tell my father that the city was not the place for me? What would I have learned from that other than how to prove my father right once again? If I can make the trip home on the land, by myself, showing I can survive on my own, then maybe he will finally respect me for the man I am."

The two companions sat in silence for a few moments. "Why are *you* doing this, Jo? I mean, one way or another I have to get home and this is the path I have chosen. But you didn't need to come with me."

"Ever since my mother died my father has treated me like a piece of china. Everything I do he is certain I am going to hurt myself. He never lets me do anything on my own. I want to take chances and learn from my own mistakes. I guess going with you on this trip is my way of showing him that I can look after myself too."

SEVEN

The trio had been traveling for several days now. Jo had proven much more capable in the woods than Napachee had ever expected. She pulled her own weight and was even making the trip enjoyable. Her knowledge of the area was much more in-depth than Napachee's. He was an expert on the tundra, but in the forest he learned to rely on her knowledge.

Napachee was, however, learning to read every sign and every trace of the animals in the forest. He could feel danger before it presented itself, and his keen senses seemed more in tune with the animals than a weapon to be used against them.

When he did kill, it was for food only and he felt pride in his skill and ability to hunt the Inuit way. Each time an animal was taken, Napachee carried out the traditional practice of thanking the animal for giving of itself to keep them alive.

Napachee and Jo felt guilty for the worry they may

be causing their parents and had been tempted to try and draw the attention of low-flying planes on several occasions, but the need to complete the journey on their own had driven them on.

❆

Jarvis drew hard on his cigar and, opening his mouth, slowly let the smoke drift upward to the ceiling. He watched as it curled around the florescent light, in a smog-like cloud. His hands confidently clasped behind his head, he tipped back in his chair and propped his feet on the desk. His uplifted arms revealed sweat stains and his ample belly sagged in the middle of the v shape his body formed. Crumbs from a recent indulgence still rested there.

With sudden violence, he bolted upright and slammed both fists into the accumulation of paper and garbage on the desk! He swept his arms wildly across the surface sending paper in every direction. His blood-shot eyes stared at the wall across the room. The wall was bare, but in his mind he saw a polar bear cub and a young Inuit boy who had eluded his every attempt at capture.

He had flown with James Strong for many hours over many days looking for the teenagers and the bear cub. He had watched as James studied the land with eyes full of despair and worry, searching for any sign of his daughter and the boy.

He had watched the land as well. They had

received reports of possible sightings, but when Jarvis had investigated these on foot, they had proven false alarms.

However, his survey *had* revealed the tracks of the bear cub, Jo and Napachee heading northwest. They knew exactly where they were going and would head toward the Mackenzie River and try to take advantage of this route to the ocean. He had told James and the others that the boy was confused and the tracks he had found indicated that the boy and girl were to the east, beyond Deline and Great Bear Lake. He had not mentioned that they were traveling with the bear.

Jarvis had informed the others who continued the search that he would not join them. Now removed from the official search, he was ready to carry out one of his own.

❄

The rivers, streams and lakes were ever plentiful and the food that they provided sustained the group as they continued on their way. Jo was amazed by the crisp fresh air and the clarity of the waters they encountered. To sit and watch trout, pickerel and pike swim by in large schools was a first!

One afternoon, as they approached the marshy edges of a lake, she stopped and gazed across the water at the beauty around her.

"It's strange, the way they sun themselves, isn't it?" Napachee said. "I have seen land-locked Arctic

Char do the same thing near Cambridge Bay."

"What are you talking about?"Jo asked.

"Over there." Napachee pointed to a shallow area full of weeds and vegetation.

Jo fixed her gaze on the points poking above the surface. These "weeds" were in fact the dorsal fins of fish laying in the warmer shallow waters. She had always enjoyed camping with her father and going on field trips, but she had never seen anything like this. Once they had gone camping in northern Alberta with her two cousins (who were boys) and her father had given them more responsibility than he had her. If only he could see her now!

She missed her father and regretted the worry he must be feeling, but she knew she would make this journey and see him again. Perhaps this trip would make all the difference.

Napachee was inspired by the beauty of these lands as well, so different from where he had grown up, but still so beautiful. They were, however, hard to navigate. With plenty of water and muskeg, there were always detours and although he knew the general direction in which he wanted to move, he was never quite sure they were on course. As far as he could tell they had been travelling for four days. The crash had taken place near Fort Providence on the north side of the Mackenzie River. He wanted to keep them near the river so he continued to move northwest in the direction of Wrigley and Tulita, situated on the banks of the river. There were mountains and many miles to cover. If they were to make the long journey, at some point they would need help. Many of the people from Tulita had ties with those from the Mackenzie Delta. Perhaps they would assist the wayward travellers.

As they made their way overland they encountered many animals; animals Napachee sensed almost before he saw them. When he had been out on the land with his father he had never felt this way, never been as close to the land as his father had been. When he did come across animals they moved about him as if he were one of them, not a predator but a trusted friend.

The past few days had been hot and Hagiyok periodically had to stop to take a lengthy soak in a stream or lake. He was not used to these temperatures and would have been more in his element sitting on an ice flow or resting on a snow bank.

In the dry heat of a northern summer, fires can often be started by lightening strikes. They had seen lightening in the distance on several occasions and one afternoon Napachee caught the faint smell of smoke. The smoke became stronger and soon visibility was very difficult and the air hard to breathe.

Napachee led Jo and Hagiyok on with urgency because he could feel the intense heat of the fire building around them. His instincts told him to move quickly to the north and he was right! A river lay ahead of them. Napachee hoped that the fire had not spread to the other side. In the smoke, he couldn't see across, but he knew they had to swim.

"I'm a pretty good swimmer," said Jo, reading Napachee's mind. "Will Hagiyok follow?"

"Polar bears are born swimmers," Napachee replied. "They even have webbed feet, which is what I could use now. I'm not a very good swimmer at all."

"Don't worry, I'll be right here if you need help."

Jo and Napachee waded into the river. With some hesitation Hagiyok followed and soon took the lead. The river was wide and the crossing took much longer than Napachee had anticipated. Just as Napachee thought fatigue would overtake him they reached the shallows of the other side. They lay on the shore for a long time regaining their breath.

"Let's keep moving," Napachee said finally. "I don't know if we'll encounter fire on this side as well, but even if it isn't on fire now, flames from the other side could still jump over at any moment. The more distance we put between us and this spot, the better."

As they left the river the smoke began to lessen. Napachee relaxed into the rhythm of their journey.

❈

They had now reached one of the lower mountain ranges and it was tougher going for the bear. Hagiyok was learning from the journey and no longer relied on Napachee or Jo for food, though the cub still never ventured far from their sight. It would follow closely behind Napachee anticipating changes in direction before the boy took them.

For better or for worse the raven had adopted them as well! It followed at a safe distance, but close enough to irritate Hagiyok without end. When there was food present it was always within striking range, but out of reach when the cub tried to retaliate. Despite its annoying behaviour, the raven had been a valuable ally. On more than one occasion Napachee had sensed danger and the raven had identified the source with its loud squawking.

One afternoon they neared the end of the mountain range and paused by a cool, fresh stream to refresh themselves and rest. They had been traveling since early morning and Hagiyok had found the day tiring. The cub slipped into the stream and shuddered with pleasure. Jo and Napachee lay on shore and napped.

When Napachee awoke he decided to explore a nearby cliff that dropped into a ravine. At the lookout Napachee squated on his haunches and tilted his face to the sun. The heat felt good and he closed his eyes to enjoy the moment. Suddenly, Napachee sensed, rather than heard, a presence behind him and turning slowly looked *Nodah* the mountain lion straight in the eyes. The large cat had quietly crept up on him.

At that moment the sound of rock clattering over the edge drew both Napachee's and the mountain lion's attention away from their confrontation. A Dall's sheep stood on the ledge gazing in their direction.

The mountain lion watched Napachee for several seconds before turning and quietly padding under the cover of trees.

Napachee let out his breath and slumped to the ground in relief. He hadn't realized he had been holding his breath and now gasped for air. He looked skyward as he exhaled and lowered his gaze to the edge of the cliff. The sheep was no longer there.

Napachee walked back to their temporary camp and sat beside a sleeping Jo until she opened her eyes. Napachee related the story of the sheep and the mountain lion, concluding with, "I don't suppose you believe me. I'm not sure I believe some of the things that have happened lately."

"I do believe you. You said your grandfather taught you that each person's life is foretold by the great spirits; perhaps this is your destiny. Animals seem to have some strange connection to you. I can't explain it. Your father was not wrong about your gift, only your use of it."

EIGHT

Enuk scraped the knife along the sharpening stone, over and over again. The blade had been finished for some time but he didn't notice.

"If you don't stop that soon Enuk, you will have a handle but no blade."

Enuk looked over at his wife and then down at the knife he had been working on. His mind had been thousands of miles away. He put the knife down and headed off to feed the dogs. Talik lay her *ulu* down beside the skin she had been working on and followed.

"Enuk, ever since Napachee has been missing, you have been impossible to talk to. You know I share your feelings and yet you won't talk to me. You eat little and sleep even less. I know you are trying to keep busy and settle your mind on other matters but I can also see this is eating you up inside. You can't blame yourself for what the boy did. Every father and son argue and it is never only one person's fault. I feel pain too, and we need to talk and share these feelings with each other."

Enuk carried the pails of fish and water to the dogs who noisily acknowledged his approach. He filled their dishes and stepped back to watch the feeding frenzy. He walked over to one of the plywood boxes the dogs slept inside and sat down. Talik followed and stood silently beside him.

Enuk finally spoke. "Yes, Talik, I do blame myself. If I hadn't pushed the boy so hard maybe he would have come to me instead of running away. I only wanted what was best for him and I know as well as you do that the city can be a very hard place for someone from the North. There are so many traps in the big city. I have to accept the fact that the world is changing around us and a teenager will want to change with it."

His eyes met his wife's and he nodded his head knowingly. "I didn't try to influence the boy, I tried to force things on him and that was wrong. But I wanted to show him the things that my father showed me. Napachee never had time to listen and that was so frustrating. We have tried to teach our children what is best about our culture and where has it gotten us? Over the last year Pannik has stopped speaking our language altogether and Napachee refused to speak unless there was no one around to hear him because he was embarrassed. He once told me that we would have to speak English if we wanted to learn anything or get anywhere.

"When I went south to look for Napachee I felt

helpless! I don't know that land like I know our own. All I could do was follow the others as they lead me along like a lost child. I know that James Strong is a good man and even though the government has called the search off he will continue to keep looking, but at some point he will stop. What will we do then? Napachee was just a boy."

"Napachee is alive." Enuk looked up at these words from his wife. He began to smile.

"He is not a boy, Talik, he is a man. He knows how to hunt and to survive. He is on his way home!"

Taking his wife by the hand, Enuk began to walk back to the house.

"We must phone James Strong and make sure the search continues!"

＊

As the days passed, the three companions journeyed through the final low mountain range and came upon the Mackenzie River. It flowed from the south to the Arctic Ocean.

"Are we close to Sachs Harbour? Is this the last leg of the trip?"

"It's not quite that easy, Jo," Napachee sighed. "As long as we follow the river we kind of know where we are. My guess is that we are somewhere near Tulita right now. The problem is the river doesn't go straight to the ocean. The Mackenzie River is the largest river in Canada. It will start to twist and turn. If we could fly like that silly raven and go straight as an arrow, it would take us only a couple of days to cover the ground it will take us a week to cover by following the river. The further we go north the more channels we will hit. Then the Mackenzie Delta spreads out into so many channels and streams that you can get lost in minutes unless you know your way. It is the second largest in the world! We are going to need help!"

Napachee fell silent and stared across the river.

"Then we'll just have to get the help we need and finish the trip as we had planned!"

Napachee could see the determination in her eyes.

"You're right. I knew we would need some help sooner or later. We will follow the river and hope we come upon Tulita soon."

The next few days of the journey were easier as the trio entered lower marshy terrain. Jo watched as the bond between Napachee and Hagiyok continued to grow. When the cub was perplexed by the strange world it had been forced into, Napachee would take the place of its mother and show it how to cope. With a glance from Napachee Hagiyok would head off in the right direction. When the bear cub sensed another animal or what it felt to be danger, without external signals Napachee knew it too.

❋

This part of the river did not bend back on itself as much as Napachee had thought it would and he felt with each step they were closer to home. By his calculations they should also be getting closer to Tulita. Tulita was on the banks of the Mackenzie, as long as they followed the river they couldn't miss it. They would have to make contact with someone there if they were to continue.

They had been living on fish and small game that Napachee managed to spear or snare. Jo had recognized some plants that were edible including some types of mushrooms, but they needed more than that if they were to cover the great expanse of land that lay before them.

These thoughts occupied Napachee one sunny morning as they walked through a thinly wooded area not far from the bank of the river. They emerged from the wooded area they had been traveling through and began to cross a large open field of wild grass and moss.

Napachee became aware of the sound of a plane not unlike ones they had heard before, but this time something worried him. Jo could hear the sound now too and stopped to look skyward.

The sound changed as Napachee listened, and he realized it was not a plane but a helicopter. He looked to the horizon and saw a speck which began to grow larger with alarming speed. Napachee looked at the other side of the clearing and realized that it would likely overtake them before they could reach cover.

"Go!" he shouted at Jo as he broke into a run. He charged ahead across the clearing. Glancing back,

Napachee saw Jo fall and raced back to help her up. She winced in pain as she rose to her feet, only to fall to the ground on an injured ankle that wouldn't support her weight. Placing her arm over his shoulder Napachee hopped ahead as fast as he could with Jo beside him and Hagiyok loping behind. They were still yards from cover.

"Over here!" Napachee snapped his head sideways trying to locate the stranger's voice. He saw nothing at first but then spotted a boy about his age peering above an indentation in the ground. He was waving at them furiously! Picking up Jo, Napachee rushed the last few feet to the hollow and threw himself in. Hagiyok was close behind and they landed in a gasping heap at the bottom.

With the sound of shallow breathing in his ears Napachee strained to hear the helicopter, expecting it to land close by.

It never happened. The helicopter flew overhead and continued on to its destination. Napachee slowly let out his breath in relief.

Napachee could feel Jo moving behind him. Hagiyok stumbled to get up while Napachee quickly scrambled to help Jo up.

Jo pushed herself to a sitting position and started to wipe the dirt off of her face. Sputtering, she spit a mouthful of dirt and sand at Napachee's feet.

"My name is Alfred," the boy said holding his hand out to Napachee. "I live in a community not too far from here called Tulita," Alfred said pointing. "We should go before it gets too late or before the helicopter gets back.

"The white man and the helicopter have been here for the past week. He never says what he is looking for, but he heads out every day to look again. He is going to the community of Norman Wells tonight, but he may return. The white man will be in our village until late afternoon. It is just over this rise. Once he leaves we will continue."

They all settled in the shade and Alfred continued to talk. "Two sleeps ago one of our elders had a dream. In this dream he saw a white bear and a boy, running through the wilderness. The elder said that the boy had a special purpose and when he arrived it would mean well-being and good fortune for the Sahtu Dene who would help the boy and would be blessed as a people for it. The elder also said that a girl followed the boy and the bear. This girl had a head of fire."

Napachee and Jo looked at each other in disbelief, but said nothing.

That evening a strange procession quietly made its way into the community of Tulita. Alfred ran ahead and by the time the others arrived many people had gathered to meet them.

Napachee sat on the porch of Alfred's house and stared out across the Mackenzie River. Many of the homes were made of logs and sat in the trees high on the bank overlooking the river. The homes were otherwise very similar to those in Sachs Harbour.

He could see how much the land meant to the Dene of Tulita, as it did to the Inuvialuit and Inuit. The river was a source of life and Napachee watched as boats came and went and people traveled to check their nets. Alfred's father drove Napachee and Jo around the town later in the evening explaining to Jo that Tulita meant "Where the rivers meet."

The water of the Bear River was clear and pristine where it flowed into the larger, muddier Mackenzie. A huge section of rock on the other side of the Bear River had shapes on its surface. Alfred's father followed their gaze and told them it was called "Bear Rock".

Jo and Napachee were given a special place at Alfred's house for the night and a small feast was held in their honour. They had felt it best to keep Hagiyok away from the community itself so had placed the cub in a dog pen just outside of the community for the night.

They sat around a fire high on the bank overlooking the river and enjoyed the company of their hosts. As Napachee witnessed the song and dance of these people, he felt he was nearly home.

After a few moments, one of the elders came forward to tell them the story of the giant "Yamaria".

"Many years ago the great giant Yamaria created the Mackenzie River and its surrounding lakes which formed as he walked in the shape of his mighty footprints. The giant was chasing three beavers and when he caught them he placed the three beaver pelts on Bear Rock where you can still see these markings today. He then traveled up the Bear River to Deline where he placed his staff in the river. A rock in the shape of an arrow still stands in this place where the Bear and Mackenzie rivers meet. For this reason, Bear Rock has special meaning and spiritual power for the Mountain Dene."

Alfred sat with Jo and Napachee as they enjoyed the evening. Napachee grew quiet, wrestling with his thoughts.

"I know the elders believe in the spirits and that animals and people can have special powers as well, but it is difficult to believe *I* could be special in this way."

Alfred turned to Napachee and said, "I believe that something special is happening. You shouldn't take aboriginal beliefs lightly. I am convinced that the dream of our elder was true and you are here to prove it. I used to question the legends and stories that our people told, but there was wisdom in their words."

After a brief pause Alfred continued. "Several years ago there was a very bad forest fire not too far from here. With each day it moved closer to Tulita so they started to evacuate the town. Most people knew that the fire was going to destroy the town and all would be lost. As the fire burned it reached Bear Rock, but never came any closer! It changed direction and eventually the firefighters and nature put it out. The elders believed that the power of Bear Rock protected us and turned the fire away. Some people would say it was just coincidence, but I have never questioned the beliefs of my elders again."

As he slept that night, Napachee dreamed he had entered the world of spirits where mist swirled around his head. Animals ran past him and he saw fires and strange creatures he had never seen before.

When he awoke the next day he remembered fragments of the dream and set about studying it for signs of what lay ahead.

NINE

After being blessed by the elders of the community and being given gifts for their journey (as was the custom) Napachee, Jo, and Hagiyok were taken down river by boat.

Hagiyok settled quietly on the floor of the boat. Jo's ankle was still sore from her fall and she was grateful for the boat ride and a chance to heal.

In a few hours they arrived at Fort Good Hope on the banks of the Mackenzie where the Hareskin Dene held another celebration in their honour.

After the festivities Jo decided to explore the town on her own. She walked along the gravel roads that wound throughout the community; few vehicles or people passed. From the main road through the centre of town she walked past fish drying on racks and smoke houses where caribou meat was prepared. In backyards skins were stretched on racks to be used for clothing or crafts.

Jo took a path from the main road down to the

river banks. She marvelled at the beauty of the land she knew was so important to these people, amazed at the silence and wilderness just moments from the houses on the main street.

Meanwhile, Napachee came upon the church he had so often heard his father speak of; it was famous across the arctic for its beautiful paintings. He opened the front doors and without taking his eyes off the ceiling slowly lowered himself onto one of the old wooden pews. The entire interior of the church had been painted by priests who had served in the community. The ceiling was a blue sky full of stars. Pictures of saints, Jesus and the Mother Mary adorned all of the walls.

Later, they sat in the huge log building that served as a community hall and listened as the Fort Good Hope drummers played and sang.

Jo asked, "Is Sachs Harbour like this?"

"It is similar yet very different," Napachee replied. "The land itself is unlike this, but its importance is the same. When I was young and lived in Cambridge Bay, many people worked for the government and had day jobs in the community. When the warmer weather came they would set up tents outside town at sites they had held for years. Every morning they traveled in to work and at night returned to their camps. For most aboriginal people of the North the land and their traditional way of living gives them both energy and happiness. If they are away from the land too long, they feel the need to return to it to regain their inner strength.

"I know my father is happiest when he is on the land. He feels a part of it. I did, too, when I was young, but somewhere along the way I lost that. Seeing the city and making this trip, it is as if that part of me has returned."

❄

The time had come to move onward, and the three travelers were taken by boat further north. The country changed as they went. The trees were smaller and the air was cooler. The river banks were very high and two days later they came to the place where the great Mackenzie and the Red River met. Here on the bank, beside the Red River, sat Tsiigehtchic. This was the land of the Gwich'in Dene.

To leave Tsiigehtchic it was necessary to take a ferry or travel on the river by boat to the Dempster Highway and drive north to Inuvik or west to Fort McPherson. They decided to take the ferry to the west side of the Mackenzie River and take the highway on to Fort McPherson. There they would take the Peel River north to Aklavik deep in the heart of the Mackenzie Delta.

They chose this route because the alternative, Inuvik, presented too many problems of secrecy. It was a large community so it would be impossible to keep Napachee, Jo and Hagiyok out of sight and unnoticed. Napachee feared that if they traveled to

Inuvik they may encounter Jarvis and word would spread before they could finish their journey alone.

In Tsiigehtchic a light snowfall was on the ground. They were informed that not only had summer come late, but winter was coming early. The warmer weather had been brief and apparently the colder weather was already settling in. If they wanted to get to Aklavik by boat they would have to depart quickly.

Being careful to conceal the three travelers under a tarp, they were taken across the ferry by truck and driven on to Fort McPherson. Here the Gwich'in took Hagiyok, fed the cub and put it in a dog pen near the banks of the Peel River.

Jo and Napachee stayed with respected elder Johnny Charlie in Fort McPherson. Johnny Charlie had once been Chief of the Gwich'in and would take Napachee, Jo and Hagiyok on to Aklavik when they were ready.

While they waited to continue their journey, Johnny Charlie took Napachee in his scow on the Peel River to show him the surrounding area. He pointed to a large rock on top of the river bank.

"That is Shildii Rock. There is a story about the rock which has been passed down from generation to generation. There once was an old man who lived with his wife, three sons and daughter. The daughter, Ts'eh'in, was said to possess magical powers.

"In summer they fished and camped at Scraper Hill, Deeddhoo Goonlii. One day the old man spoke to his boys. He said, 'My children, I am hungry for meat.

NAPACHEE

I want food. Go to the mountains.' The boys left and the daughter remained behind with the old man and her mother. The boys traveled to the mountains west of Fort McPherson, the Richardson Mountains. They were gone for some time.

"The mother knew of her daughter's powers and spoke to her. 'My daughter, soon your brothers will be returning. When they do, you must not look at them and you must not say anything.' At that time, around Shildii Rock, there was nothing but barren land. There were no willows on the hill. From where the girl stood, if she looked down river, it would be easy to see her brothers returning. Her mother knew this.

"Soon she became very lonesome for her brothers and was anxious for them to come back. Although her mother warned her, she forgot what she was told. One day she saw her brothers walking toward her.

"'Mother, my brothers are coming home!' she exclaimed. All at once the three brothers turned to stone, three rock pillars in a row. The dog which was with them also turned to stone. This is Shildii Rock.

"Their mother was cooking bannock when this happened and it is said that the bannock, too, turned to stone. Today if you look carefully at Scrapper Rock, you'll see the stones used to bake her bannock. When people pass Shildii Rock they leave something of their own out of respect for the rock."

❋

There was snow on the Richardson Mountains and it would be on the ground in Aklavik. With Johnny Charlie as their guide, they headed down the Peel River in his scow toward Aklavik. The trip would take less than a day through the Huskey channel and the Black Mountains into the Rat River.

"This section of the Rat River is very famous," Johnny Charlie told them. "Years ago a man they called the 'Mad Trapper of Rat River' lived here. He started to steal food from the traps of the Gwich'in who lived in this area and they complained to the R.C.M.P. The R.C.M.P. went to visit him at his cabin and he shot and wounded one of the officers. While the Mad Trapper was trying to get away he killed another policeman in the chase. They finally managed to trap and shoot the Mad Trapper, but never found out who he really was."

"I learned about the Mad Trapper in school," Jo said. "Who would have believed I would be on the river near his cabin some day."

The day grew late and the air cold. When they finally reached Aklavik it was almost dark and hard to see. Hagiyok was left outside the community and the other two companions were whisked to a home where they would be lodged for the night.

Ice had started to form on the smaller channels of the Delta. It would not be possible to complete the trip by boat. It was decided that Napachee, Jo and Hagiyok would stay in Aklavik until they could safely continue by snowmobile. They would make their way to Tuktoyaktuk.

Aklavik lay at the foot of the Richardson Mountains in the heart of the Delta. Both Gwich'in Dene and Inuvialuit lived there. The travelers had been kept as hidden as possible, but rumours had spread.

The R.C.M.P. stationed in Aklavik were sure to spot unfamiliar faces if Napachee and Jo ventured out in public. They were forced to limit their time out of doors and had to sneak out of the community to visit Hagiyok and explore the area.

Jo was taken to hunt caribou, make bannock, tan skins and learn some of the other skills of Gwich'in women before they left.

When they were ready to go they mounted the snowmobiles which had been volunteered by members of the community until the they could be returned.

Hagiyok loped behind Napachee and Jo as they headed off through the Delta. They carried their gifts of provisions, including gas and other supplies, on sleds the Gwich'in had provided.

Napachee no longer slept outside in his sleeping bag, but in one of the canvas tents made in Fort McPherson and seldom needed anything to provide additional heat other than the Coleman stove for cooking. The journey was faster with snowmobiles, but they still had to wait for Hagiyok and it was much colder now with the trees quickly thinning out and no longer providing shelter.

"Over there!" Napachee shouted. Opening the throttle on his snowmobile he sped towards a stark, lone shape on the horizon. He did not stop until he reached the large figure, made from stones piled one on top of the other.

"This is an Inukshuk," he told Jo. "It has been used by my people for centuries to guide our travels. They are also used to mark the path of caribou herds and caches of meat left behind to be collected on return journeys. They have been here, and it has remained all of this time to show us the way."

Though relieved to see a talisman of good will, they were soon distracted by the sound of a helicopter speeding in their direction!

Napachee could hear the helicopter's engine getting louder behind him. He saw the snow jump just ahead, and he realized that someone was shooting in his direction!

Hagiyok was some distance ahead of Napachee now. The bear jolted to a sudden stop at the top of a rise on the open land ahead. Seconds later Jo came to a sudden stop beside Hagiyok and looked back. As Napachee joined them on the rise he saw why they had not continued their flight.

The Arctic Ocean, unfrozen and forbidding left them with nowhere to retreat! They must be further west than Napachee had bargained.

Napachee turned and felt the blast of wind push the hair from his forehead. The helicopter was settling down a short distance behind them. Jarvis jumped from the pilot's seat and ran in a crouch toward the retreating trio. As he moved closer he slowed to a deliberate walk and unslung his rifle.

Napachee, Jo and Hagiyok had backed onto the thin ice that lined the shore of the ocean and had nowhere to go. Jarvis slowly walked onto the edge of the ice, raised the rifle to his shoulder, and aimed directly at Hagiyok.

The ocean ice under Jarvis exploded! Jarvis was thrown backwards and with one brief cry of terror he was tossed into the water and disappeared below. Bubbles continued to rise where Jarvis had disappeared and his rifle slowly drifted to the surface.

Napachee moved over to the edge of the ice and knelt down. Jo dropped to her knees and felt for a brief moment that she would be sick to her stomach. She looked up at Napachee, but could not speak.

"He is dead."

Jo moved off of the ice and wandered back to her snowmobile. She covered her face with her hands and began to sob. Napachee stood by helplessly.

"There is nothing we could have done. Jarvis would have shot Hagiyok. The water is very cold and the ice couldn't support his weight. He was sucked under by the current and there was no way we could have saved him once he went under. It's over now."

Jo knew Napachee was right but she had never witnessed anyone's death and the shock was almost too much for her. Napachee sat down on his snowmobile and stared out across the water.

"Where is Tuktoyaktuk?"

Napachee looked up and could see that most of

the color had returned to Jo's face.

"It is to the south east. We somehow managed to go too far west and north. It means we are going to have to do some backtracking, but it shouldn't take us too long to get there.

"I was thinking about a friend of my father's, Wilfred Pokiak, who lives there. He used to run a schooner in this area and he may be able to help us."

Jo nodded and started her snowmobile.

"Let's get going Napachee. I want to get as far away from this place as possible."

TEN

Napachee and Jo waited outside Tuktoyaktuk until complete darkness settled over the quiet community. Napachee didn't want to be spotted, but they needed help. He felt the need for extra secrecy after their encounter with Jarvis. Being this close to home there was a chance they might be recognized.

Leaving Hagiyok just outside of town, Napachee and Jo crept carefully through the rows of houses. They were just two other people in parkas on snowmobiles, zipping through the darkness.

Gathering his nerve, Napachee slowed and passed a woman walking along the road. He asked for directions to Wilfred's house. Jo kept her hood up and head bowed as they pulled away and moved along the snow-packed gravel road. She could see the odd spark flash off Napachee's snowmobile skis where they struck gravel.

Leaving Jo with the snowmobiles, Napachee walked to the door, opened it and stepped in. In the

North if you were a friend you didn't need to knock.

"Hello!"

Napachee recognized Wilfred's voice from the other room as he took off his boots. Wilfred visited Napachee's family many times in Sachs Harbour.

"Hello," Napachee called back in Inuvialuktun.

At the sound of his own dialect Wilfred stuck his head around the corner. His eyes opened wide in surprise and he moved toward Napachee to hug him.

"The missing one has been found," he finally said in a soft Inuvialuktun whisper. Wilfred was only 5' 5" tall but what he lacked in height he made up for in girth. He was naturally stocky and years of hard work on the land had made him muscular. His face was weathered and dark from his years on the snow and ocean and he had a huge moustache that he often greased and curled up at either end. A deep scar ran from the outside corner of his left eye to the top of his left ear. On another person the scar would have been sinister or frightening, but on Wilfred it simply made his smile appear warmer.

Wilfred led Napachee to the living room and sat him by the wood stove stoked with driftwood. Napachee curled up closer to the fire, and taking a cup of tea began to speak. He spoke in Inuvialuktun and recounted the entire adventure to Wilfred. At many points Wilfred shook his head in disbelief or uttered a solemn "Eeeeee" in agreement.

"So where are the bear and the girl now Napachee?" he asked as Napachee neared the end.

"The bear is just outside of town where I told him to stay, and Jo....Oh no! Jo is waiting outside!"

Napachee rushed to the door and gingerly peered outside. Jo stood inches away with a blank look on her face. Her eyelashes were frosted and her nose shone a bright pink. With an angry glance Jo hurriedly pushed past and entered the house.

"I'm too cold to even ask why it took you so long to let me in."

Wilfred met her, and with a smile helped her off with her parka and led her to the warmth of the fire. Handing her a cup of tea he settled into his chair.

"I'm pleased to meet you Jo," Wilfred smiled. Jo wasn't sure whether it was the fire or Wildred's friendliness, but she felt warmer already. The three sat in silence, relaxing and watching the flames.

"So where do you go from here Napachee?"

"You are the only person I know that can get us to Sachs Harbour by water."

Wilfred sat back in his seat as Napachee continued.

"I know your schooner has not been used for many years, but I also know you have kept it as good as new. You have navigated the sea ice for many years and I know you can get us to the island without help from others."

Wilfred remained silent for a few moments and then began to speak. "*The Sea Otter* has made many a difficult trip. It is a fine ship, with a proud history. It first belonged to a respected elder originally from Alaska who traveled these waters and then settled in

Nunavut. He was related to your father. If there was to be a fitting end to your journey I am sure it would be with *The Sea Otter*. I have treated it as a parent would treat a child and although I have not used it for a few years I have looked after it.

"The fact remains it would take days to make her seaworthy and if anyone finds the helicopter they will start to search for Jarvis in this area. That will make our task all the more difficult."

Wilfred could see a look of disappointment cloud the faces of both of his guests. "If the three of us start to work tonight, however, I believe we can have her in the water the day after tomorrow."

Jo leapt from her chair and gave Wilfred a big hug.

"Easy now," Wilfred laughed. "Even Napachee here didn't squeeze me that hard."

The next few nights were busy ones. Jo helped where she could and took food to Hagiyok who remained outside of town. When they needed a break, Wilfred showed Jo and Napachee some of the area. There were three volcano-like formations nearby called "pingos". They had cores made of ice and had been forced out of the ground by pressure in the ice below. Wilfred showed Jo and Napachee where years ago people had created storage freezers, by digging out rooms in the base of the pingos, to keep things cold in the summer.

Tuktoyaktuk had once been a booming oil town and they also saw several abandoned oil rigs and living quarters that had been used for large crews of men.

❄

On the third evening in Tuktoyaktuk Napachee sat beside Wilfred taking a break.

"We are ready to leave. Our work is done, the ocean is calm and the temperature is right. We will need to use the motor, but the sea ice will be steady so our trip will be smooth. Ask Jo to take the bear along the shore, so we are not spotted, and we'll be off."

Wilfred remained with the boat and reviewed everything they had done to get ready for the trip. The schooner was in perfect running order with the work they had completed over the last few days. They had plenty of supplies aboard and the trip should only take a few days.

Wilfred looked up from his final preparations and spotted Napachee, Jo and Hagiyok approaching.

"You said a bear *cub* Napachee. Hagiyok looks more like a full grown male!" He stepped aside as the three made their way on board. Wilfred tentatively reached out as Hagiyok passed, and gently touched the bear's back. Without stopping Hagiyok looked back and opened his mouth. Shaking his head, Wilfred untied the ropes and hopped on board.

The first night and day of the journey went even better than expected. There was no wind and the strong engine pushed the reliable craft through open water and small groupings of ice. The skies were clear and the air grew increasingly cold.

"We have had company for the last hour," Wilfred

informed Jo and Napachee. He pointed across the bow and they saw the form of a large Bowhead whale.

"*Arqviq* has been keeping us company."

Arqviq wasn't the only animal they saw as they traveled. On several occasions they encountered pods of Beluga whale as well.

"Do you still hunt whales?" Jo asked.

"The Inuvialuit are allowed to hunt a quota of twenty *Qinalugak*, Beluga whale, each year. But we never harvest that many. There are almost too many *Qinalugak* right now. They are doing very well, but the food they eat is getting less plentiful due to their large numbers. The whales' blubber contains vitamin C. Eating the blubber, *muktuk*, helped our ancestors survive. Today we keep some small whaling camps at traditional sites, but kill very few whale."

"Have you ever seen any narwhal in this part of the arctic?"

"*Toogalik* the narwhal is only found in the eastern arctic."

As *The Sea Otter* neared Sachs Harbour things took a turn for the worse. The wind had picked up, shifting all of the sea ice closer to Banks Island. Napachee could tell by the grim look on Wilfred's face that things were not going the way he had intended.

"How bad is it?" Napachee finally asked.

"It's bad enough," replied Wilfred. "But it's not impossible. I'm guessing from the direction of the wind that the ice ahead, in the direction that would lead us to Sachs Harbour, will be packed together and almost impossible to navigate. I am going to shift direction and give this side of the island a wide berth to head around to the north. There is a harbour on that side which I am sure will be open. I know of this harbour because it is named Sea Otter Harbour."

It was late the next morning that *The Sea Otter* pulled into Sea Otter Harbour. Once they had gained the north side of the island the going had been trouble free. Wilfred and his passengers stood on the shore.

"You have a gift Napachee. You must learn what it's for and use it for a purpose that will benefit our people and others. Jo you are a brave girl and a strong person to have come this far. Use the strength you have gained. Reclaim your home Hagiyok. This is your land too."

Wilfred turned and hopped back onto the schooner. "Say hi to Enuk for me Napachee," Wilfred smiled. Jo and Napachee waved until the schooner was out of sight.

ELEVEN

Winter had returned to Banks Island. The air was fresh and the land covered with a hard layer of clean, crisp snow from the relentless wind. Their feet crunched as they moved further away from the shore.

The land looked barren and desolate without trees or vegetation, but a texture of light Jo had never encountered before haunted everything she saw.

Napachee spotted an Inukshuk and knew they did not have far to go.

Hagiyok, too, could smell familiar scents.

Napachee stopped and surveyed the land ahead of them. "Do you see those rocks in the distance?"

Jo followed his gaze and nodded yes.

"Take a closer look."

Jo squinted her eyes and concentrated on the dark objects on the horizon. The longer she stared the more it appeared they were moving.

"My eyes are playing tricks. They look like they are moving across the side of that hill."

"They are moving. They are muskox! Our word for muskox is *Omingmak*. We are down wind so if we take our time and walk slowly we should be able to get pretty close."

They slowly walked forward and the dots on the horizon began to take on a different shape. Jo had seen pictures of muskox, but they were even more impressive in the flesh. They didn't stand as tall as she had imagined and were much woollier than she had pictured. Their horns swept forward in awkward swirls, and their coats shook in the wind. They looked like a cross between prehistoric woolly mammoths and buffalo.

They were able to move along the rise in the land and stay out of sight until they were very close to the animals. As they came into full view of the herd, the lead bull snorted. The animals quickly moved and formed a circle with their backsides toward the centre and their heads facing out. The babies were protected in the centre of the circle.

"They do this when they are threatened," Napachee said. "If there are only two muskox on their own, they will stand rear to rear to face whatever is threatening them. There are many on Banks Island."

Napachee was getting more excited with every minute and wanted to press on. As they continued to walk he recognized landmarks from dozens of hunts he had been on with his father.

"Look over there!" Jo whispered, grabbing Napachee's arm and pointing ahead to the right.

Napachee squinted. There, far ahead, a hunter was silhouetted against a drift in the snow. He was lying on his belly, rifle in his hand. He crawled across the snow, intent on something beyond the drift. He reached the top of the drift and stopped to take aim.

Napachee, Jo and Hagiyok moved quickly, but silently across the snow at an angle that allowed both the hunter and the hunted to be in view. They moved parallel to the hunter to see what lay ahead.

A large polar bear stood beyond the drift taking a leisurely sun bathe in the crisp arctic snow. It was up wind of the hunter unaware it was being watched.

Napachee glanced across at the hunter and saw him prepare to fire his gun. He removed his fur mittens and swung them behind his back on the strings that held them together around his neck. He moved the rifle into place and sighted his quarry through the scope.

As Napachee watched the ritual he had seen dozens of times before he heard a series of soft grunts beside him. He glanced down at Hagiyok and saw something he recognized in the bear's eyes. He whirled around to look once again at the hunter.

Napachee began to run!

He watched his father settle deeper in the snow to get a comfortable shot. Enuk stared at Hagiyok's mother as she sniffed the afternoon air.

"Nooo!" Napachee cried, running across the snow.

His father was up wind and Napachee knew his voice was falling on deaf ears. He could hear his heart pounding in his head and he could not breathe.

Napachee's father continued to stare through the sights of his gun.

Napachee saw Enuk close his other eye and wait to hear the report of the gun as it fired.

Enuk lifted his head away from the sights and lowered the gun. He did not know why he could not pull the trigger. He stared at the large female polar bear ahead of him and then slowly stood up. He turned away from the bear and looked directly into the face of Napachee!

Both father and son stood staring at each other. The rifle slowly dropped from Enuk's hand and as if in a trance he began to walk towards his son.

Napachee broke into a run once more and rushed into his father's arms.

Enuk embraced his son and rocked back and forth. He looked into Napachee's eyes as tears began to drift down his cheeks.

"I am home Father," Napachee whispered in Inuktitut. "I am home where I belong."

Hagiyok charged at his mother who began to lick his face.

Napachee led his father over to where Jo had been standing some distance away.

"Hi. I'm Jo."

"I know who you are," Napachee's father said. "I met your father when I was in Edmonton to help with the search and I know he is going to be very happy when he finds out you are alive! We will call him as soon as we return to town."

Enuk placed his hand on his son's arm and Napachee turned to face his father.

"I am sorry I have been harsh with you," Enuk said.

Napachee tried to speak but his father raised his hand for silence.

"I have been a hunter as your grandfather was and his father before him. I have seen our world changing and have tried to ignore it. What is right for me is not necessarily right for you. You have been proud and strong to make this journey back to our land, and if it is truly the white man's world that interests you then those are the feelings that you should follow."

Napachee smiled at his father and nodded his head. "I do not want to be a part of the city. I have learned that I am not meant to be a great hunter like you. We are great hunters. We must protect that, our language and all of our customs, but we must also work with the other peoples of the North *and* those from the South if our culture is to survive. I know I want to play a part in this."

Enuk smiled and nodded to his son. "Let us go home," Enuk said softly.

As they walked toward the *komatik* Napachee stopped and turned, looking for Hagiyok and his mother. He could see them slowly moving off across the snow. Hagiyok stopped and looked at Napachee. He lifted his nose and sniffed the air, taking one faltering step forward. Hagiyok's mother gave a low grunt and with one last glance, he moved to join her.

"Goodbye my brave friend," Napachee whispered. Jo placed her hand on Napachee's shoulder.

"You are welcome here, Jo," Enuk said warmly. "The fact that you have made this journey with Napachee shows that you respect the land and the way of the Inuit and Inuvialuit peoples. You will be a special guest in our home until we can get you to your father."

With a soft click of his tongue, Enuk set the dogs in motion. Napachee and Jo jumped onto the sled and Enuk hopped on in front of them. The sled swooshed across the ice in the fading light of an arctic evening.

NAPACHEE

NAPACHEE

GLOSSARY

Aklavik   A community located in the Mackenzie Delta. Aklavik means "A place of the bear and grizzly".

Amoute   A special parka with large hood used to carry babies and small children.

Arctic Char   Salmon-like fish known for their fight who run the waterways to the ocean to spawn each year. They range in size from 2 - 30 pounds.

Arqviq   Inuktitut for "bowhead whale".

Dene   The name preferred by aboriginal people in the North who are neither Inuit nor Inuvialuit, and may be called "Indian" or "First Nations" elsewhere.

Doge   Slavey for "Dall's sheep".

Enuk   Traditional Inuit male name meaning "person".

Fan Hitch   A method of hitching dogs to a *komatik*. It allows dogs to spread out in a fan formation in front of sled as opposed to a single line as with other sleds.

Gwich'in   The Dene people located in the Mackenzie Delta, Northwest Territories. The name can be translated with several meanings, including "living there," "the place where you live" or "people".

Hagiyok   Inuktitut for "strong one".

Hareskin Dene The Dene people located in the Sahtu region or Mackenzie Valley of the Northwest Territories.

Igloo   A snow house built in a dome shape from blocks carved out of the snow piled on top of each other.

Inuit   Eastern Arctic aboriginal people formerly called "Eskimos" who live in the territory now called Nunavut. The name translated means "the people".

Inukshuk   A figure composed of stones piled on one another used as a landmark by Inuvialuit and Inuit. It is also used to mark the path of caribou and the locale of caches of meat.

NAPACHEE

Inuktitut   The language of the Inuit, sometimes written using geometric symbols and syllabics or using Roman orthography.

Inuvialuit   Western Arctic aboriginal people who live in the Northwest Territories. The word translated also means "the people".

Inuvialuktun The language of the Inuvialuit, which is rarely written.

Inuvik   The main center of the Western Arctic with a population of approximately 2500. Inuvik means "the place of man".

Itsé   Slavey for "moose".

Iqaluit   A community in the extreme Eastern Arctic and the capital of Nunavut. Iqaluit means "where the fish are".

Komatik   Inuit for a flat, low sled, also called *Qamutigruaq*.

Mountain Dene The Dene people also found in the Sahtu region or Mackenzie Valley.

Muktuk   Whale blubber eaten by the Inuit and Inuvialuit peoples for its taste and vitamin C.

NAPACHEE

Napachee   Traditional Inuit male name.

Nodah   Slavey for "mountain lion".

Northern Lights Otherwise known as the Aurora Borealis. Greenish, blue lights that appear in the northern night sky.

Nunavut   The official territory created in 1999, which borders the Northwest Territories to the west and Alberta, Saskatchewan and Manitoba to the south. It was formerly part of the Northwest Territories and now recognizes the distinct society and lands of the Inuit. The name means "our land".

Okpik   Inuktitut for "snowy owl".

Omingmak   Inuktitut for "muskox", a large pre-historic looking animal with shaggy hair and curled horns that roams wild before being herded and killed for meat.

Pannik   Often pronounced "Bunnik". Inuktitut for "daughter".

Qanuripit   An Inuvialuit greeting meaning "hello".

Qinalugak   Inuktitut for "beluga whale".

NAPACHEE

Quaq　　　　　Raw, frozen fish or caribou.

Slavey　　　　The Dene language spoken in regions of the Northwest Territories including the Sahtu, Mackenzie Valley. It is spoken by the Hareskin and Mountain Dene.

Talik　　　　　Traditional Inuit female name meaning "arm".

Tasó　　　　　Slavey for "raven".

Toogalik　　　Inuktitut for "narwhal", a whale with a unicorn-like horn on its head found in the Eastern Arctic/Nunavut.

Tsiigehtchic　A community formerly known as Arctic Red River. Situated where the Mackenzie and Red Rivers meet. It means "Red Stones" in Gwich'in.

Tuktoyaktuk An Inuvialuit community on the coast of the Arctic Ocean, Beaufort Sea. It means "where the caribou are".

Tulita　　　　The community formerly known as Fort Norman. It means "where the rivers meet" in Slavey.

NAPACHEE

Tundra   Northern barren land without trees and minimal vegetation, covered in permafrost.

Ulu   A knife used by the Inuit and Inuvialuit shaped like a half moon used to skin and slice meat.

ACKNOWLEDGEMENTS

This work would not have been possible without the help of many people. Thank you to my wife Carla, for all her support and encouragement. Special thanks to David and Annie Akoak, Lyall and Mary Trimble and Loretta Trimble, Angela Grandjambe, Stella Beyha, Tom Beaulieu and Betty Firth without whose help *Napachee* would not have been possible.

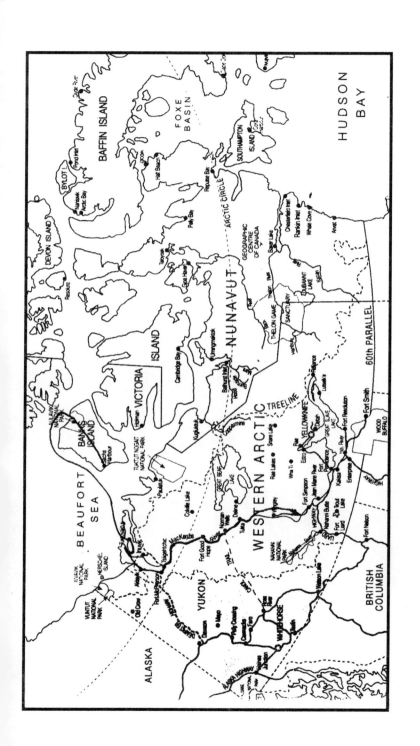